Set in vivid, exotic lo
from the Arabian des
powerful anthology of
a place in which pain a
nightmares, obsession a way of life, and death.

The Songbirds of Pain confirms Garry Kilworth in
the front rank of British writers.

'arguably the finest writer of short stories in
Britain today in *any* genre.' *The New Scientist*

'*The Songbirds of Pain*' is excellently crafted . . .
Kilworth is a master of his trade.' *Punch*

'a fine collection by a British writer who shows
great versatility and invention . . . it's a pleasure
to read such a solid and varied collection.'
Starburst

'a bony-handed clutch of short stories, addictive
and hallucinatory.' *The Times*

THE SONGBIRDS OF PAIN

Stories from the Inscape

GARRY KILWORTH

UNWIN
PAPERBACKS

LONDON SYDNEY WELLINGTON

First published in Great Britain by Victor Gollancz Ltd, 1984

First published by Unwin® Paperbacks, an imprint of
Unwin Hyman Limited, 1988

UNWIN HYMAN LIMITED
15-17 Broadwick Street, London W1V 1FP

Allen & Unwin Australia Pty Ltd,
8 Napier Street, North Sydney, NSW 2060, Australia

Unwin Paperbacks with Port Nicholson Press Ltd,
60 Cambridge Terrace, Wellington, New Zealand

British Library Cataloguing in Publication Data

Kilworth, Garry
   The songbirds of pain.
I. Title
823'914[F]   PR6061.I39
ISBN 0–04–440217–1

Printed and bound in Great Britain
by Cox & Wyman Ltd, Reading

*to Caribbean friends
and sunny days*

CONTENTS

INTRODUCTION

A short story should be as precise and accurate as an acupuncture needle in hitting the right nerve. There the analogy stops, for the nerve should jangle, not deaden. Since the target is a different one each time, uniformity of type is not possible in a collection such as this, but there are linking aspects which, though vague, I hope will serve to smooth the reader's path from one story to the next. The settings are often exotic and sometimes oriental: they are drawn from cultures I have experienced and experience is too valuable to be wasted. The characters are usually ordinary people in extraordinary circumstances. Occasionally, where extrapolation is more important than either character or setting, such as in "Oubliette", these are not readily identifiable, but even here the subconscious must draw on reality, and familiar, lighted areas emerge from the dark background. What I hope the reader will find is that each story can be viewed from more than one perspective: "Sumi Dreams of a Paper Frog", for instance, could all be taking place in the narrator's head, with no reference to external events; or the outside world is "real" and has a warping effect on the protagonist's mind.

Also, though the plots differ in their courses, there are common themes. Many of the stories deal with the soul — that is, not the Christian concept of the soul exactly, but the spirit that is fashioned from the personality: conscious, sub-conscious, memory, emotions, and all the other abstract qualities that make the human psyche. "The Invisible Foe" concerns a soul caught between ambivalent loyalties; "The Rose Bush" a soul tormented by an unfulfilled and desperate desire to bear a child; "The Man Who Collected Bridges" an exotic soul stained by contact with commonality; "The Dissemblers" is about the marriage of souls. These are all contemporary themes, albeit dressed in the richly-coloured robes of science fiction and fantasy.

Immortality is another connecting theme — "Almost Heaven"

and "Lord of the Dance" are two different approaches to the same house. In these two stories the subject is dealt with overtly, but it is also there in "Scarlet Fever" and, in a darker, racially-inherent sense in "God's Cold Lips". "Blind Windows" and "Let's Go to Golgotha!" stand a little apart from the rest, as does the title story, "The Songbirds of Pain".

Apart from these connecting threads I hope, on another plane, that these few stories satisfy, at least to subsistence level, a certain taste for a sense of wonder. What is intended is that they should move the emotions and through them reach that soft spot in the intellect which allows entry to the story form known as "science fiction". These tales span ten years of writing in a chosen genre which for many years I admired as a reader and am now proud to be part of as a writer. I believe in science fiction as a serious literature form which is swimming against a tide of ignorance (not in the derogatory sense of the word) and a natural distrust of the unfamiliar. However, any new, perceptive readers to science fiction may quickly realize that it is only the props that seem unacceptably strange — props that allow a greater penetration and deeper journey into the world of the imagination — not the subject matter, nor the characters.

Garry Kilworth
1984

THE DISSEMBLERS

"Yea, though I walk through the valley of the shadow of death ..."

Christian teachings still run thickly in my blood. My new religion, a mere two years old to me, is like an adopted child: dear because it is mine by choice, not accident. But, yet, like an adopted child it can never be truly part of me. It is a grafted branch, well-taken and, indeed, an extension of me, but not inherent. Thus, those phrases from my childhood learnings spring to mind more readily in crises, than do the new words, though I love the latter more. Those others were with me from birth, and now I am nearer to death than the beginnings of my life, I sometimes panic. Will I be ready? Will I be ready? Or will they scream "Dissembler!" in my wake as I try to gain entrance into a world I barely believe in?

"You must be Orget. I'm Jane Reece."

I looked up from my newspaper to observe a tall, elegant blonde woman in a safari outfit. The clothes were obviously Zandra Rhodes. The woman inside them finished by a Swiss school.

"It's rude to stare, Mr Orget."

"I'm sorry. Please sit down." I placed the four-day old paper on the table before me and nodded to her companion, a thickset man with square, tan features. He was about two-thirds her height.

"You too, sir, whatever your name is."

"His name is Chota. He's a deaf mute," she replied for me, taking one of the rattan chairs. Chota followed her example. Around us coffee was being served in glasses the size of egg-cups. I signalled the Arab waiter. He saw my three fingers and gave the slightest of nods, not even turning his head. Through the glassless window behind my guests I could see the mountains of the

Hadhramaut rippling in the heat waves. Before them, the dust-rock desert furrowed unevenly by deep wadis. Brown kite hawks created invisible whirlpools in the air above. I turned my attention back to my visitors.

"I expected *you* yesterday," I said, "and him not at all."

She stiffened, two red spots appearing on her high cheekbones. "Chota is here for a reason. It's nothing to do with protecting me, Mr Orget . . ."

"Ray."

". . . though he's quite capable of doing so. He's from Papua. A forest Indian."

"Well, you look as though you usually know what you're doing. Did you fly up from Aden? In the DC3?"

She nodded. "The one wallpapered inside with a rosepattern design." It was a serious remark.

"There is only *one*. Bit of a hairy ride, isn't it? I suspect the wallpaper is to hide the cracks in the fuselage . . . it gets a bit bumpy over the Radfan hills . . . the thermals. Tends to shake up the superstructure." I could see my frivolity was having very little effect and immediately abandoned it. "Let's talk about why you're here," I said.

The coffee had arrived accompanied by three glasses of water. The waiter placed them on the table. I paid him immediately, the coins clattering on the small, brass tray. Jane Reece was staring at the thick, black sludge in her coffee glass.

"I don't want this . . ."

"Then don't drink it, but we're in a coffee shop. It's paid for. Now, I understand you want me to find your husband for you. That's what the letter said."

Her blue eyes observed me coolly. I could see a strength in her face I was not used to in one of her class. Then, mentally, I reprimanded myself for my prejudice.

"I haven't heard of anyone called Reece in the Hadhramaut," I continued, "and I would have done so, if he were here. There's not that many whites in the area."

"His name is John Freeman. I didn't take his name when we married and he didn't ask me to."

I held up my hand as her mouth began tightening.

"Please. You needn't go into details. John Freeman I have

heard of. He was at the Consulate in Sana'a, wasn't he? Then he came down to the Hadhramaut last cool season. I understand he discharged himself from the diplomatic service . . ." The Papuan Indian momentarily distracted me by dipping his finger into his coffee. After licking it gingerly, he took another dip and grinned at me with small blunt teeth. I smiled back.

"Friendly guy. Is he a tracker? You'd have been better with a Yemeni or an Adeni. There aren't many jungles in South Arabia."

"I don't need your sarcasm, Orget, just your knowledge of the local geography. Chota has a special job to do and what it is, is my business, not yours. You won't *trick* me into revealing what he's here for. You'll know when I'm ready to tell you."

A hot breeze came in through the window and lifted a few wispy strands of her hair. She was wearing it tied up with a yellow bandana and I was about to say something banal, like, "You look beautiful when you're calm," and then remembered in time that macho males had been out of fashion since Hemingway's heroes fell from grace, and in any case, I was too old and tired. Well, perhaps not too *tired* but it was a good excuse for not attempting something at which I was bound to fail.

"Fair enough Jane . . . Reece," I added. "We'll try and find your husband for you. In my engineering days I drilled half the local desert looking for oil I never found. A man should be easy. At least he won't be hiding *underneath* the sand. Do you prefer horses or camels?"

"Horses."

"And a thousand wasn't it? Riyals, that is."

"It was seven hundred to look and three when we find him."

"*If* we find him."

"I didn't come all this way just to go home with my tail between my legs. We'll find him, one way or another."

"And when you do? What then?"

"That's where Chota comes in." And for the first time she smiled.

We met the next day and arranged enough provisions at the village to last us several weeks. I explained to Jane Reece that I knew the general whereabouts of her husband and that his location would at least be confined to one of fifty places. "He's got to live near a well," I said.

"What about food?" she asked.

"If he's got money, that'll be no problem. Other well-users will sell him food as they pass through. And anyway, there's gazelle and small game." I began to check our own provisions. Sugar, tea, raisins, flour ... We were going into the empty quarter from Shimab, where I would have to rely on reports from strangers. Hopefully Freeman would not take too long to track down. Then I could get back to my wife in Shimab. I had not told Jane Reece about my wife because, to use Jane Reece's own words, it was none of her damn business. We were ready to set off just before noon. The horses stood waiting nearby. I unrolled my mat, took out my beads and knelt in the direction of Mecca.

"What are you doing?" asked Jane Reece in a voice that suggested I was about to take part in some revolting perversion.

"I'm about to say my prayers. I'm a Moslem."

"Oh."

"You don't have any objections to Islam, do you?"

"Plenty," she replied, "but I won't let them interfere with the expedition."

"The women?" I said.

"The women," she confirmed, "and the disgusting, barbaric practice of circumcision on small girls ..."

"Islam is beautiful," I said, "it is people that are ugly." Then I ignored her and all about me to contemplate Allah, the One God, and the Prophet, peace be upon him. The strange thing was, as a young man I had never been particularly religious. It was a woman who had been responsible for my conversion. They would never have allowed me to marry her unless I was a Moslem. Once the rituals obtained a hold on one's soul however, they were difficult to shed. They were as addictive a drug as qat grass, which I had also taken to, since settling in the Hadhramaut. I knew that Jane Reece considered me one of those peculiar whites who have "gone native" but I was not going to explain my complicated reasons to her. What her Papuan shadow thought, I had no idea. The whole alien scene must have been totally bizarre to him, yet his impassive face registered nothing. He was probably storing all these wonders of humankind to mime before a camp fire in his native forests. (. . . And then this old whitey goes down on his knees and starts waving his arms at the sun, while the woman walks around him slapping the side of her boot with a short whip . . .)

The wind-blown dust and grit bit into our shins as we made our way among the foothills. Diurnal temperatures at sea level were around 150 Fahrenheit, nocturnal they were still over a hundred, yet when we went up into the mountains the waterbottles froze solid. Jane Reece had made no murmur of complaint since we had started out, three days before. She had seen black scorpions, sand-snakes and camel spiders as big as soup plates, but she just clenched her teeth and swatted at them with her crop. The privation in the empty quarter is not a pleasant experience and though she protected as much of her skin as she could, her milky complexion suffered under the harsh sun. I felt sorry for her but she would have hated me for it, so I kept my pity to myself.

On the fourth night out, at the well of Jebel Rakmel, we made a fire and cooked a lizard I had caught. She chose it as the moment to begin telling me about her husband and why she was searching for him. The story made me sick with apprehension.

"My father has been in the diplomatic service since he left university in 1922 and there was no reason why John should not take advantage of that. I persuaded him to take a post that daddy found for him in Paris. John worked there quite happily, until he was sent to Singapore to negotiate on behalf of a Briton there who had been convicted of smuggling narcotics. They still hang people for drug dealing in Singapore. John failed to obtain clemency and had to witness the execution.

"When he arrived back in England he was very shaken. Shaken, I suppose, is an understatement . . . he was deeply disturbed and began to develop an obsession with death — especially death by hanging. Books on capital punishment began to arrive by post in batches. John would take these packages to his room and lock the door, spending hours at a time, presumably studying them. Of course, I was aware how unhealthy it was and contacted the family doctor but each time he called, John would either laugh it off or treat him brusquely. John's whole demeanour altered.

From a fairly passive but optimistic personality he deteriorated into an intense, pessimistic individual. He became hollow-eyed and pale, and rejected any sort of approach by me which might interfere with his new 'interest'. Finally I broached him on his reasons for his passion with death. I told him that I was jealous of anything that took up so much of his time and he agreed to talk about it.

" 'I want to look over the edge,' he stated, enigmatically.

" 'Over the edge of what?'

" 'Death. I must see what's on the other side.' There was little excitement in his tone but there was an earnestness I had not witnessed in him before. We were in our bedroom at the time — I was preparing for bed and feigning interest in my appearance because I hoped it would encourage him to disclose more if I did not appear to be concentrating on him completely — and he paced up and down behind me as I sat at the mirror.

" 'I believe,' he said, 'that if a man could take himself to the edge of death . . . yet still remain on this side, then he could observe the naked soul . . . supposing it exists.'

"To my credit, I did not call the doctor immediately. I allowed him to finish his explanation.

" 'I've been reading about Newgate prison . . . about the triple tree — that was a sort of three-cornered gallows at Tyburn where they could hang nine people at a time. The hangman was always called Jack Ketch and he hung the criminals for at least half-an-hour before allowing them to be cut down. This was in the days before dropping the malefactors to break their necks. They were usually hauled up slowly from the back of a cart. Occasionally . . . just occasionally a man or woman would still be alive when friends cut them down.

" 'One of these people, a man called Half-hanged Smith, recounted his feelings on being taken to the very point of death.' He picked up an open book, which rested on the floor on the side of the bed, and began to read.

"*When I was turned off (hung) I was sensible of very great pain, occasioned by the weight of my body, and felt my spirits in a strange commotion, violently pressing upwards. These having forced their way to my head I saw, as it were, a great blaze or glaring light, which seemed to go out of my eyes with a flash — and then I lost all sense of pain. I saw my soul rising upwards into the ether — then I was cut down and begin to come to myself, the soul returning, the blood and spirits forcing themselves into their former channels, put me, by a sort of pricking or shooting, to such intolerable pain that I could have wished those hanged who had cut me down."*

"That night I told John he had to abandon his lunatic studies or I would have him committed to an asylum. He looked at me as if I had just betrayed him — a sort of hurt, bewildered expression — but, *you* understand Ray, I had to shock him out of it. I *had* to be blunt and honest, not kind, and to prove it to him, I telephoned our doctor there and then to arrange an appointment with a psychiatrist. John just stared at me with that helpless expression still on his face. Then he stuttered something about being sorry, and, yes, he would get rid of the books the following morning. Naturally, I cancelled the doctor's appointment immediately. Afterwards we made love — as well as we've always done." She hesitated, then nodded, "I tell you that so you'll realize we were reconciled."

"What happened next?" I asked. Her eyes were glistening in the firelight. I think she was upset but her voice was clear and even.

"Outwardly, he seemed to have put his obsession aside, but secretly he had applied for a post in the British Consulate in Sana'a — Ray, I'd like to ask you a direct question. Do you find me attractive, I mean, do I repel you in any way? Please answer honestly." I thought over the answer for a full two seconds.

"I think you're one of the most exciting women I've ever met." My answer was sincere.

"Thank you," she said quietly.

After she was asleep, I sat up and stared across the fire at our Papuan companion. He gazed back at me placidly.

"I wonder what a man who has witnessed his soul looks like?" I said softly. "Does his body blanch, to become white as an albino's? Does it become brittle, hard, like a diamond, with no feelings evident? What do you think, Chota?"

His broad face creased a fraction and there was a hint of a smile just below the surface.

"I think," I continued, "that a man who has seen his own soul, would have to be mad. I think that John Freeman is *already* mad.

I think he is as cuckoo as an early spring. *Crazy*. Savvy?" I tapped
the side of my head. Suddenly the smile was there, fully, and the
two rows of small teeth shone white in the firelight. I nodded,
returning the smile, then lay back and stared at the stars,
wondering why, as I lived longer, I should be dragged deeper into
this morass of strange human activity known as the "search for
truth" by others of my kind. Around me I could hear the desert
wind whispering dust into the dry shrubs: the insect world toiling
amongst the shale. This was no Sahara, with high golden dunes
adding majesty to an empty quarter: it was a rocky, grey volcanic
area, as dirty and depressing as a disused railway yard. This was
no place to search for the truth, to discover one's eternal soul.
Something scuttled amongst the rocks. I murmured two *suras*
memorized from the Koran, and then promptly fell asleep.

In the arid wasteland there is not a great deal to occupy one's
attention. The scenery is endless, formless and dull. Only our eyes
were visible from beneath the swathes we wore to prevent the
evaporation of our sweat and we allowed the horses to maintain a
slow walking pace in order not to tire them. Only the wind offered
any variation of elemental mood. The occupation of one's mind
was dependent upon material fed into it around the evening
camp fire. During the long days my imagination reconstructed
the scaffolds of eighteenth century England, where the theft of
single shillings was enough to ensure their constant usage. Jane
Reece had read some of her husband's books and she told me of
men, women and children who went to the gallows dancing, crying, singing, shouting abuse, shivering in terror, silently dignified
. . . every emotional display of which a human is capable. She told
me of Jonathan Wild, the self-styled Thieftaker General, responsible for many such hangings, and who was himself finally
"turned off" by Jack Ketch. She told me of the "Ballad of the Long
Drop" that concludes: "We dropped her, for we drop them
straight, for love as well as hate". These images haunted my
waking hours as well as my dreams. I filled the void, the naked
countryside of the empty quarter, with pictures from my head.
There were trees springing out of every rock and from those trees
swung corpses of various sizes and either sex. She made me a
child again, with new nightmares and new dependencies.

For the next two weeks we travelled from well to well asking questions of strangers. I would exchange greetings with hill tribesmen, then ask them in Arabic if they had seen a crazy European, a mad Christian, in the vicinity. "Are you of the Faith?" they would ask suspiciously. When I confirmed I was, they said, "But aren't *all* Christians crazy?" After which I would get my information, Or not, as the case was.

We moved cautiously, for the hills were the haunt of lean, fierce nomads, not instantly hostile but easily provoked. In such harsh conditions hot tempers lived just below the surface and violence was a spontaneous, irrational and unpredictable reaction to minor irritations. "I am against my cousin," went the local saying, "but my cousin and I are against the stranger."

The two aspects of the journey which bothered Jane Reece the most were firstly not being able to wash herself or her clothes to the degree of cleanliness she considered acceptable, and secondly, my *affaire* with Islam. She would stamp around me impatiently during morning prayer and afterwards would remark derogatorily upon the intelligence level of devout, pious idiots that believed in magic. I tried to explain that, despite the bad publicity Islam had received over the last decade, it was essentially a simple working-man's religion and providing one carried out the five main duties required of a follower, a place in Heaven was assured. Much of what she disliked about it did not stem from Islam itself but from the various cultural roots of countries in which it was practised. The only true religion was atheism, she said. Then, to underline her contempt, one morning she situated herself between my prayers and Mecca, stripped completely, squatted, and washed herself over a bowl as I did my Salaams. She made her point: she had destroyed my religious concentration with a carnal display. She was magnificently disdainful. The two-fingered iconoclast. She could sneer like no other woman I had ever met and it made her absolutely desirable.

Finally our search took us to a village by a small artesian well at the foot of the Sallala mountains. I made enquiries in the suk and was informed that a man, a foreigner, was living in some caves about thirty minutes' ride from the village. Although the conversation had been conducted in Arabic, Jane had caught the gist from the gestures.

"He's here, isn't he?"

"We don't know it's him. Let me go and see this man first. It might not be John."

She stared into my eyes. "Are you afraid of what condition you'll find him in? You must know my threshold by now. I'm difficult to shock." I looked away from her. Chota was squatting on the ground by a patch of dates that had been left to dry in the sun. He picked one up and crunched it between his teeth before spitting it back out with a look of distaste.

"Let me go first," I repeated. I wanted to meet John Freeman without Jane there to affect his personality. From her reports he sounded a weak man, with barely enough willpower to run away from stronger forces. But a personality is not immutable; it changes shape according to the influences to which it is subjected. John Freeman might well have been a strong character, outside of Jane's shadow.

"We'll go with you," she stated. "You can go in first if you think you're going to find him in horrible circumstances — but I'm sure he'll be all right. He's not the sort of man to mutilate himself. He doesn't like deformities."

"It's a cave, in the hills," I said, and we collected our horses from the boy who was watering them and rode off in the direction indicated by my informant in the suk.

The caves looked as though they had all been inhabited at one time. Their entrances bore the marks of having been fashioned into doorways. There were about two dozen of them on a ledge several hundred feet up, accessible by a steep path. Behind them a range of dark red mountains flowed in petrified waves. We left the horses at the foot.

"Wait here," I ordered. One of the higher caves had a hessian curtain hanging over its entrance and I guessed this was the one we wanted. I pulled the hessian aside and entered.

The atmosphere in the cave was stifling. I could see little at first, the only light coming from a foul-smelling candle on a small rock shelf at the rear. Then, gradually, I perceived some furniture: a chair and table, a raffia sprung bed, and right at the far end, as deep as the cave went into the rock face, a weird contraption of pulleys, ropes, beams and levers. At first glance it resembled one of those early wooden printing presses one sees in museums, except that it was too tall, much too tall, and there was a sinister import to the angles of the beams and the way the rope stretched tautly between them. The whole device appeared to be bolted into the rock wall for support.

I breathed deeply, trying to find some air that was not thick with the heavy, musty smell which filled the cave. There was a movement a few feet to my left and a man stepped out of a shadowy recess into the candlelight. We regarded one another without speaking for a few moments. He stood straight and lean, and wore a dark ragged beard, encouraged by long, unkempt hair. His eyes were deep in his face, but clear and bright. There was a strong line to his cheekbones and his shoulders were firm. From his physical stance, he did not look a weak man. His appearance implied confidence and assurance. I guessed he was weak only in comparison to his wife. Nor was there any indication that he was insane, but I had yet to hear him speak.

"You like my machine?" he questioned in Arabic.

I nodded. "Ray Orget," I said, extending a hand. "I've been looking for you."

He started and then said, "My God, English? I thought you were an Arab." I looked down at my filthy and dust-grimed hands. Beneath the dirt and headcloth I could have been any nationality. I looked up again. "I've brought your wife. She's outside."

"Jane? Here?" Panic sprang into his eyes and he looked like a cornered wild creature about to bolt. Then he seemed to get control of himself and slumped down in the chair.

"I suppose she wants me to go with her," he said, gloomily.

"I've no idea what she wants. My instructions were to find you, that's all. What happens now is between you two."

"Between us two," he repeated, but there was more than a suggestion of irony in his tone.

"She's concerned for you . . . For your state of mind."

"I know, that's why I came here." He slammed a fist down on the table. "My God, is there nowhere I can go to escape her?" He stood up and waved his arms. "Up a mountain in Tibet? Down a trench in the Pacific Ocean? Where? Where can I go and not be found out? This is one of the most godforsaken, loneliest places on Earth, and *still* she finds me."

"She's a very determined woman," I said stiffly. "And I might add, a very beautiful one."

He looked at me with a peculiar expression on his face, over his left shoulder, for a few moments, then shook his head. "No. You're probably too old, more's the pity. Yes, she is beautiful . . . and her determination is part of that beauty. I once thought I could never live without her. I was right. I can't."

"But . . ." I indicated that he was here.

"This?" He let out a short, humourless laugh. "This is not living. *Existing*, yes, but not living."

"Your choice though."

"Yes, my choice. But it seems as though I do not have the freedom to choose. Okay," he said in a resigned voice, "tell her to come in. I'll talk to her."

Before I left I said, "Have you used that thing back there?"

"So she's told you about my . . . hobby? Several times. I had it constructed by a local carpenter. The wood wasn't easy or cheap to come by. However, it works well. It's me that doesn't function properly. I lack courage, Mr . . . ?"

"Orget." Evidently he forgot names quickly.

". . . consequently, I always pull the releasing lever before time. *Time* is that moment when I can stare Death in the face, yet still turn around and walk away."

"So I understand."

"No, you don't understand. No one does, but then I'm not looking for understanding. I don't give *that* . . ." He snapped his fingers. His voice was dry and crisp. "All I want is to be left alone to experiment. That's why the entrance is covered. The locals wander up here sometimes, out of curiosity. I can't discourage them physically . . . wouldn't want to. So I have to hide."

"You actually hang yourself."

"For a few seconds." He lifted his beard and I could see red weals around his neck. I must have winced because he laughed.

"Is it . . . painful?" Despite my abhorrence of his particular form of insanity, I was morbidly fascinated.

"Of course it is. It hurts like hell. But I can't think of any other method of doing it without leaving my body mutilated or my internal organs damaged. I have to do it, Mr Orget. Make no mistake about that. When you've seen a man hang, as I have, you'd know by his face that there is a point where the expression of pain changes to one of wonder . . . then the muscles slump into death. I have to reach that point. I *have* to. Before the man becomes the puppet. All our lives we live in the shadow of death. I must see what casts that shadow."

I took a long look at the bizarre contraption that reared like a giant praying mantis, throwing its own scaffold shadows over the cave wall, and inwardly shuddered. I could imagine the noise of creaking joints, the sound of stretching rope, as his body hung from the thick topbeam. What frightening, taut trip-wires were there in my own brain waiting for a specific event to trigger them with a delicate psychological finger? That intricate device, the human mind, with its multiplicity of traumas, its complexities of disturbances, its fine networks of nerves, was my inheritance as well as his. Was it possible that one day I would want to witness my own psyche in ascendancy?

Freeman was studying my face with an expression I could only attribute to some ugly demon that swam in his spirit and rose occasionally to the surface.

"You want to see me use it," he said. It was not a question. He strode quickly to the machine, muttering, "Maybe with an audience . . . ?" Before I could stop him he had stepped up on to a small platform and pulled a noose tight around his neck, taking up the slack on a wooden windlass.

"Freeman . . . !"

"Quiet !" he silenced me curtly. The platform flipped downwards with a *snap* that made me jump. The rope tightened and his face seemed to swell to twice its size, as if it were gorged with blood. His eyes grew wide and lost their natural lustre. In his right hand he grasped a short lever.

During the thirty seconds he hung before me, his limbs as limp as rags, I heard the candle sputtering away his life. In the fetid atmosphere of the cave I had the fancy that I could smell Death coming, creeping in like an evil insidious wind from the cracks in the rock walls, from beneath the ancient stones, to claim a deserter to its cause. Thirty seconds ... thirty years. And all that time there was a sound coming from his mouth like a dog would make with a bone stuck in its throat. Then I heard the wooden ratchets slip and he fell the six inches to the floor, the windlass clacking and spinning on its axle. He had pressed the release lever. He groaned, squirmed for an instant, then reached up slowly to his throat to loosen the noose. I left the room quickly and returned to Jane Reece and her primitive Indian.

"Please pay me my three hundreds riyals. I want to go. He's in there, believe me."

"I believe you, Ray, but don't leave us now. We have to return ..."

"What's Chota doing here?" I asked, bluntly.

"I think you've guessed that. John is a born failure. It doesn't lower his stature in my eyes because I can see other qualities in him that are just as important, but it's a fact. I knew he would not be able to do the thing he wants to do ... he hasn't, has he?"

"No. He hasn't," I said, quietly.

"I couldn't beat this obsession, so in order to save John, I made a decision to join it. In order to help him, I've brought Chota, who is an expert in death. John may not be able to bring himself to the point where life crosses death — but Chota can do it for him ..."

My stomach turned at the thought of it. She was right, I had had a hunch what Chota was for, but to hear her expressing it coldly and, I suppose, logically, made me feel ill.

"The Papuan Indians torture their enemies," she explained, "by bringing them continually to the very edge of death, but never allowing them to slip over ... if they did they would lose them and the whole point of the exercise is to make your enemy suffer. They use the garrotte, which I believe is similar enough to the hangman's noose to satisfy John's ... requirements. If John refuses to come back with me to be treated, I shall allow Chota to ... to give him what he wants. Hopefully his mind will then be scoured of the insanity that's trapped within it." She paused. "Will you wait?"

Like a fool I said, "Yes," but my mind was in a turmoil and she had more hold over me than she imagined. "I'll wait. Aren't you afraid that the cure might be more fatal than the disease?"

"Chota knows what to do and how to do it. I have complete faith in him. His tribe have been doing this sort of thing for centuries."

That night, I believe a man was taken to the edge of a cliff and looked down upon the rocks of Death below. Then the man turned and walked away. From my camp just below the cave I could hear the terrible sounds that accompanied the experiment above me. I did not know until later that he had had a companion as I tried to ignore the pattern of noises which attend a strangulation. A sequence that begins with a sharp *"Kahhh"* like a baby's cough; then the slow rattle of phlegm in an old man's throat; then, finally, a terrible silence. Silence can have a sound too, if the ears are pressed hard enough against its thin shell. Finally, I took my horse and rode away from them, down to the desert. I could not stand to listen any more, despite my promise to Jane Reece. I ran. My imagination was full of horrible scenes of people being hanged, pressed under blocks of stone, stretched out under a blazing sun with tight shrinking rawhide collars, crucified, cut in a thousand places, stretched on racks and wheels, keelhauled, immersed and near-drowned, sliced into ribbons . . . there were a thousand ways to bring someone to the point of death. The human mind has been remarkably inventive throughout history in finding them out. I slept feverishly that night, with pictures of blades, ropes, and engines of metal and wood spinning in my brain.

The next morning I was woken by a rough hand on my shoulder. I sat up quickly and found myself staring into the ravaged face of something that had once been human. Its features were as twisted and swollen as a gargoyle's, the beard and hair a shock of white. Red eyes glared from deep pits of pain. I shouted, knocking away the hand.

"It's me, Freeman." The voice was so cracked and inarticulate I hardly understood the words.

"Freeman?" I cried, wildly. "What . . . ?" Then I remembered. The crippled figure crouched before me was fresh from the world of suffering and . . . death. "Did you . . . ?"

"Yes! Yes! I saw." There was an inflexion in the tone. A rising note implying excitement. "You must sell me your horse. Where do you live? No, I'll send it to Aden. You can collect it there. *Please*. The animal."

"Take it," I said. "And water. You'll need water. Is she following?"

"Not yet." He began removing the mare's hobble with inept, trembling fingers. I sprang up and helped him. Then I had to lift him into the saddle.

"Where will you go?"

"Anywhere," he replied. "I must get away. I must go." There was an urgency behind the words which disturbed me. I grasped his ankle.

"Before you leave, what happened? What did you see?" I was eager to know what scenes his madness conjured for him under duress.

"Death. I saw death." There was a thin line of saliva running from the corner of his mouth and I wondered whether I had done the right thing in giving him the horse. In one night his hair had lost its colour and he had assumed the appearance of an old man, wracked with arthritis.

"What did it look like?"

His eyes were damp. "Pain. I never felt such pain before — not physical suffering but an emotional, spiritual hurt, my very *self* was torn out of the flesh by which it was held so fast. I was forcefully wrenched away from life — a psychic experience which, dear God, I will have to go through at least once more, but next time I shall make sure it's quick — a bullet in the brain, a fall from a high place..." He gripped my shoulder and pulled me closer to him. "Imagine your veins being stripped from your body or your skin peeled away from your face, eyes, limbs... it was like that, only not flesh from flesh, but *spirit* away from body.

"Then after a long time — so very long — there came a single moment of peace and I was looking into the dark kingdom of Death. It was like... staring into a deep, black mirror... eternity dropping away before me, not beautiful but awesome, terrible in its promise of the everlasting... then the soul, reflected on the surface of death.

"Listen!" He leaned down, conspiratorially, to whisper hoarsely in my ear. "A man and a woman, when they love... when they live together, they begin to merge ... their personalities. You understand?"

"I ..."

"Yes. Their egos, their souls eventually mingle ... become one, a single entity. I saw my soul ... our soul, Jane's, mine. Together. One. A single spirit. You see, she joined me. We did it together but she ... there was only one. One soul between us."

"She joined you?" I repeated, shocked. "You mean, that Indian, Chota, took you *both* near to death?"

"Yes! Yes!" He jerked upright in the saddle, his long white hair flying wild in the dawn air. "She said if I wanted it so badly, if I could not be deterred, then she was going to experience it with me. She has courage, you see, more than I have ... yet, oh God!"

"What? Is she dead? Did Chota go too far?"

"No. Not that ... the soul. The single spirit. It was all *her*. There was nothing left of *me*." With that he gave a sobbing sound and spurred the horse forward.

I stood watching him ride away into the hills, the dust rising around him like morning mist. My body felt numb. This madman ... this madwoman. They had entered my life and shattered my peace of mind. I was a Sunni Moslem, my life running according to His plan. Kismet. I followed and was led, and had no need to torture myself with right and wrong paths. I did what was expected of me and my eventual reward would have been assured. I had even steered myself away from Shia Moslems and their fanatical, political approach to the Faith because I did not want my life to reflect the disturbances created by that sect. Now these dissemblers, these ugly pursuers of death in life had crumpled my calm, had destroyed my peace. One of them wore the mask of the curious, the inquisitive, yet all he craved was escape to another place and time, where he would be beyond reach. The other was clothed in good intentions, yet underneath was a naked lust for power, of one individual over another. Now I, too, was a hypocrite, merely wearing the cloak, the guise, of a devout man, which I would gladly have discarded if ...

... *through the valley of the shadow — I will fear no evil.*

Of course, it is not evil I fear but death itself. If my soul belonged to Jane Reece, *were* Jane Reece, completely, entirely, then I would have no fear. For John Freeman, death will now be oblivion, for he will not exist except as her and she exists only as herself. He will die and then . . . nothing. No gentle love, no loathsome hate, no indescribable peace, but more important . . . no harrowing, ugly fears.

Sometime later she came riding into my camp. Her beauty was still evident but it was warped by a new knowledge. She was not physically bent and twisted like Freeman, though there were unsightly scars on her wrists and throat. Her eyes were wide and there was a triumphant ring to her voice.

"He's been here. Did he take your horse?"

"Yes. What are you going to do now?"

"Follow him, of course."

I shook my head. "I won't come with you. For God's sakes, leave the man alone. Why hound him?"

She gave me a puzzled frown, then a small, tight-lipped smile. I knew *why*. And the knowledge, evident on my face, in my gestures, left me vulnerable to her contempt. Then she was gone, following the tracks he had left. I watched her arrogant pose as she rode high in the saddle, galloping her mount down the dark grey valley. I was sure I felt only pity for her prey. Not envy. It *had* to be pity.

THE ROSE BUSH

The porch of the farm was thick with the settling evening. They sat apart, their eyes on the descent of the light into the earth.

"I bought something, in the city," he said to her. "I want to show it to you tomorrow."

The man, wiry-strong in his forty-second year, had turned his bearded face to look at her.

She asked him, "What is it?" in a voice that revealed no curiosity.

"A bush," he answered. "I've already planted it."

She frowned slightly and said, "What's so special about it. Is it rare?"

He laughed then. A small tight laugh. "Not only rare but, we believed, extinct. Come on, I'll show you now."

There were several minutes' hesitation before her ankles appeared from beneath the skirt and she stood up. She followed the man and they walked down the path to the copse at the bottom of the garden. On the far side of the trees was a patch of open ground that would have been the North American prairie of the children — had there been any children — and on the edge of this miniature plain was a newly planted shrub. There were blooms beginning to open. The bush had been there for some time and he had waited for the first showing.

"See?" he said.

Then as she stared, he explained.

"It's what you believe it is — a rose. I planted it away from the house because of the dogs — tomorrow I'll fence it in. It's yours," he added.

She swore softly under her breath, shocking him, and then turned to go back to the house. He caught her arm.

"What is it? You always liked roses."

"Yes."

"Then what's the matter. I tried to please you. It cost . . . it was expensive. It's a new breed — hardy. A survivor of the blight. There are always survivors. I thought . . . you would be pleased," he finished lamely.

"Well I'm not. I don't like substitutes. Dogs, cats or . . . or rose bushes."

He hung his head.

"Don't you think I don't know that? You talk as if you're the only woman alive that. . . ."

"Yes?" Her eyebrows arched.

"You're *not* the only woman," he said savagely and with implied significance.

She laughed then, into his face, knowing that any bed he found outside would soon be as cold as her own. It didn't matter to her. Why should it?

"There aren't any women any more," she replied. "Only dried hags like me. . . ."

Then she strode back to the farm.

From her chair on the farm's porch she contemplated her fate and could see only a waiting death. The fate of womankind and roses had always, in her opinion, been inexplicably interwoven. At least, she modified, since roses had been a part of humanity's cultural programme.

Blake's poem, "The Sick Rose", was of course not about roses at all, but about disease.

> *Oh Rose, thou art sick.*
> *The invisible worm. . . .*

The invisible worm wielded by Man, thrusting into the rose of Woman.

> *Has found out thy bed*
> *Of crimson joy . . .*
> *. . .thy life destroy.*

Not her life, but that of the unborn. And not just Man, but perhaps both — or neither. Perhaps God or something, someone even less explicable than Him. A psychological trigger.

Take her, for instance. When she had been nineteen, he, the man who now shared her unhappiness, had sent her a dozen long-stemmed roses accompanied by a card which read: *One rose for every thirty days that we have shared together — one thought, with me remains always: may roses bud and bloom forever.* He was not a poet. The words had been hard found. There had been twelve roses in that bunch. A year of slow courtship.

When the flowers arrived, by special delivery, she had been about to sever their relationship. Instead she had married him.

Not long after that the roses began dying, all the roses, everywhere.

She believed the story in the press. The roses were withering under the onslaught of an artificial disease. An accident: the result of tests with an organic weedkiller of which they lost control. We never learn she thought bitterly. The rabbits had almost gone the same way with myxomatosis. Man is, accidently, a deliberate killer.

She believed the story in the press but she could not help thinking that, to a certain extent, she and the man had been partly to blame. They had pledged roses against their happiness — and happiness had failed them. Not because of the roses — that was a side issue in her mind and he undoubtedly did not even consider them. There were other flowers, if horticulture interested him, which it did not. He was a farmer, not a horticulturalist, although he had once grown roses for pleasure when they had been abundant.

The *real* issue had of course been, not death, but non-birth.

How she had longed to feel the weight of a child within her. Had made love to the man with joy and exuberance, knowing that the result might be a seed that grew to a small person with arms and legs; eyes, nose and mouth; hands and feet. A child. A *baby*.

The lump came to her throat and threatened to choke her. *Don't say the word. Don't think the word.* There were none now. They, those small creatures, no longer existed outside the longing of a woman's body. Think of the folding day instead. Think of . . . the new rose. The rebirth of lost living beauty.

Fireflies played like truant candle-flames among the branches of the pines and the needles of the pines fenced with one another in the spring breeze, perspiring their own particular brand of perfume into the warm air. It was a beautiful evening, full of small

birds, like inkblots on the bushes. A robin, having survived the
season of stiff water and iron-hard earth, swelled its small chest
and strutted giant-like among the radishes. Water was in plenty
and the ache for food was too old to be even a memory. Horses
could be heard in the distant fields, racing the breeze and
dancing to a music that lived in their heads. It was a peaceful
evening for the world around the farm, and happy too, for
everything but the man and the woman. For them it was like any
other evening: it was the end of one of the last days of
Humankind.

The man, beside her again, sighed and she turned to stare at his
dappled hands. They twitched and jumped in his lap — itching to
be at work and away from her scrutiny, she knew. Like two brown
and white rats they scratched into his jeans. Rats. An apt simile.
Men were like rats. He had explained that much. Rats and
children. They too had much in common. They both responded
to the same music. The Pied Piper of Hamelin was a terrible
biological safeguard buried deep within a woman's body.

He had told her that people were like the rodents the scientists
had used in their experiments. A colony is bred in a confined
area. The food and water supply is maintained and increased
with each new birth, or several births. Warmth, light, air — all the
necessities are there.

But the rats cease to breed.

The colony eventually dies when no new young are forthcoming. An instinctive mechanism within the creature operates.
Click. No more space. No more young. No more births — just a
whimpering death.

What's the use of a safety mechanism that can't be reversed?
she thought. I can see its purpose — but not its everlasting
purpose. It has killed my child. Or worse, it has never allowed my
child to be born. She felt the lines of bitterness tighten like steel
springs around the corners of her mouth.

Just then the man spoke. He had guessed the nature of her
thoughts. "Once we were over the whole Earth, and every corner
of it knew our kind. We knew no blade of grass that was not
touched by our hand, nor a beast by our foot. We multiplied . . .
and then ceased to multiply. I know the words," he said, "by heart.
But the meaning has gone from me. I *could* forget it, but you can't.

It's in your head night and day, a child, a child. . . ."

"Shut up," she snapped. "Shut up, shut up. Don't speak to me any more."

She jumped out of her seat and ran into the house. Minutes later she lay in her bed and the cycle of thoughts began again. Later the man came into the room, but only stayed a few moments, quite still in the dark, before leaving her. His footsteps sounded on the wooden porch and then were gone.

Thank God, not tonight.

The following day she walked out of the house before he woke, and went into the city. There she tried to lose her thoughts in the childless streets. Around her barren form moved the phantom shapes of an aging population. A constant reminder of a dying race. She had been a child herself when the gift of creating life was wrenched from womankind, never to be returned.

A hunched figure in a black shawl moved across her line of sight and into one of the slumhives that humped the crowded city.

Never? Never to return? The rose had returned. *She must think about that.*

A man came near her, touched her through the thin dress and murmured something unintelligible into her ear. She ignored him. The touch had been surreptitious, light. She hardly felt it. Once it would have been an underhand grabbing of her buttocks, accompanied by a lewd remark and a leer. But not now. Such gestures were futile. They had little meaning and were the manifestations of despair. The touch had been an offer unaccompanied by any urgent desire. Merely an offer. There were pairs who still tried, hoping that their particular chemistries would produce the magic combination which would result in a child.

She had been through all that.

When they had first married she had been full of hope. No children had been produced for ten years, but she and her man were very much in love. It was not possible that such love would go unrewarded. They would produce a baby, my God, without the sperm, without the ova, but from pure *love* alone. Besides, they were of the fortunate few. They lived outside the city on a farm, away from the monstrously crowded slumhives. They had space. God would be kind.

They had melted into one another each night, fearful that a critical time might be missed if they failed to make love on any single day.

And the months moved into years without the yearned-for stirrings in her body. It was then that she had run away to the city and tried the others, not caring who or why. They took her at parties and in hivecells, in barbooths and at night in the parks. Sometimes even in the alleys. There were many desperate women and only a handful of willing men. She took it where she could find it. Each time it happened, she lied, saying, *Lord it feels so good it must be this time.* But it never was, and finally, when she realized that she was not a single unit but merely a part of a writhing, serpentine animal that slithered and slipped its way in and out of itself, tying and untying a knot of white flesh to no purpose, she returned home to her own man.

They had screamed at each other and fought on that night — which ended with him taking her almost against her will. Not rape, because she had allowed it, in the end, after he had called her all those names and had ripped away her clothes. She did not let him touch her again for many months. Now she allowed him, occasionally, to enter her bed but she called out her suffering as he loved her, and he could only take the humiliation she meted out when his needs had been unsated for many weeks.

When evening came she returned to the farm and found him anxiously peering out into the half-light.

"I missed you," he said, and she saw by his face that he meant it.

He did not ask where she had been or with whom or why. She knew he did not want to hear anything that would turn the muscle of his heart another twist.

"I'll cook you some dinner," she replied. "You're probably hungry."

"Hungry? Yes," he said an an absent-minded tone. His hand rested on her shoulder as they stood in the doorway. She could feel the callouses on the palm, and the heat from his blood, through the thin material. Her breasts rose and fell steadily and she did not brush him away. She thought about the man in the street whose hand had lightly moved against her thigh and she felt sorry for them all. The men who needed sons and daughters to carry their blood into another generation.

"The rose has returned," she said. "I never thought it would." He nodded, and they went inside.

After the meal he went to bed, no doubt hoping against hope that she would join him later. She walked out, passed through the copse, and under the moonlight approached the rose bush.

Its dark blooms glistened with drops of crystal. The man had watered it before retiring and the heavy fragrance of the blossoms wafted over her. Spontaneously, she thrust her hand into its leaves and felt the scratching of its thorns. It awakened something within her, the shock of those tiny daggers biting into her bare skin.

Protection. A woman has her own devices.

She pressed her lips to the petals of a bloom. Would it stain? She recalled the deep reds seen in the evening sun the day before. Her tongue moved amongst the soft petals, gently removing the drops of liquid.

Roses had covered the farm once. Delicate hybrids that needed constant care and attention, but they had been beautiful. Their colours had crossed every boundary and she had taken them for granted.

Once again she pushed her hand inside the bush, not caring this time that the thorns raked her flesh. How did a rose feel when its secret places were violated? Perhaps that was the wrong word. The pollinating insects were hardly violators. They did their work gently, caressing the blooms with their tiny bodies, their constantly vibrating wings.

She pressed her face deeper into the flower, crushing it against her cheek and allowing its perfume to swamp her senses. The rose of a woman is not so easily crushed, she thought. It suffers the indignities of such pressures time and time again.

Her hand, inside the bush, clutched at a stem and almost without thinking she ran it down the barbed stalk. The roses were back. They had, somehow, managed to survive and propagate. Some of the fertility of this rose bush might transfer itself to her — in a hyperphysical sense. Her hand felt sticky and she realized it was bleeding. Her head spun with a thick giddiness. Opening her shirt she bared her breasts and then, gathering the rose bush in her arms she pressed it hard against her body and moved against the barbs.

When she returned to the house, she woke the man.

The following morning the man ran his fingers over her lacerated breasts and said, with horror in his voice, "Did I do that? I don't remember doing that."

"I fell," she said. "Into the hawthorn on the way back from the field. I struggled, which only made it worse. I should have . . . it doesn't matter. They'll heal. See, the scabs are forming already."

She came to him often after that, and sometimes she was bleeding from small cuts. He pitied her and tried to get her to stop wounding herself although he enjoyed having her as a willing partner in his arms once more. All through the winter her small body found its way to his bed and he loved her as he had never loved her. His questions went unanswered and soon they were unasked.

One night in February he followed her to the rose bush and witnessed an unholy scene. It filled him with anguish as he heard the incantations and saw what must have been ritual pain-inducement.

Without interrupting her he left them, the almost leafless rose bush and his wife, and stumbled back to the farm in disbelief. He said nothing to her, on her return, but loved her tenderly and with great compassion.

Why is it, he thought, that we feel we need to suffer pain in order that good may come about? She needs to do no penance. She has done no wrong. We need the gift of a child and she feels she can exchange her own physical suffering for that gift.

Or perhaps he was wrong? Maybe she had discovered there was some strange power in a rose — a fertility drug? He would let the rites continue. After all, what harm could she come to? They were only scratches.

Spring is a time when bees wander with echoing footsteps through empty honeycombs and laying chickens begin to cast reproachful looks as other eggs start to hatch.

In the spring the bush began almost imperceptibly to die. The man recognized the symptoms and knew there was nothing he could do.

He wanted to weep, for the rose as well as for the end of all his pleasure. He knew in his heart that such a relationship — the unhallowed triad — was profane and could not withstand erosion or madness for ever. Nevertheless, it was all he had — all they had. And who knew, perhaps the devil would have seen fit to pledge them a child where goodness had failed them? She would have loved it, whether it had horns, hoofs or halo. It would be a child. The source was irrelevant. The origin of the passion immaterial.

Now he had something to do. Something that crushed his soul — what soul he still owned — into a painful lump that lay on his stomach. One evening when she was asleep beside him, he left her and went into the field with a spade. He dug the bush from its soil bed and burned it in the incinerator along with every scrap of its roots. The authorities would have expected him to destroy the shrub, but that was not his main reason for doing so. It was only his excuse. He wanted to eliminate the dying object of his wife's obsession. Her lovemaking of late had begun to reflect the desperation she had shown in their earlier married years — when she had begun to lose hope. Spring had arrived, with all its other animal births, and she was still as far from pregnancy as she had been last year — and all the other springtimes of her adult life.

When the deed had been carried out he went straight to work in the fields, punishing his body with fatigue in order to atone for his *own* sin.

That evening he found her hanging from a beam in the barn. A bale of straw lay on its side only inches from her small feet.

He thought he had cried before that day but those previous tears were nothing to the dry sorrow he experienced now. He wished he *could* weep, but not a single tear came from that dreadful heaving storm of grief within him. He merely stood with his arms around her rigid thighs and pressed his face to the cold abdomen whispering over and over, "I *loved* you. I *loved* you."

When he had finished with grief and cursing God he cut her down and laid her carefully on the dusty, straw-strewn floor of the barn and went into the city. There he made a purchase and returned once again to the farm.

Under the moon that night, he dug a shallow grave where the rose had once stood and placed her inside it, gently. She stared up at him: a small, white, pathetic, once-upon-a-time creature of his life. He filled her mouth with earth and pressed the purchase, a rose cutting, in the soft soil between her lips. Then he covered the corpse with humus.

"She shall have her child," he said softly, and to no-one but the whole world. "She *shall* have her child."

BLIND WINDOWS

Quinlan's eyes were full of anger. "Do you know what the hell time it is?"

"Yes," I said. "August."

Although I had not been aware of it, I had come to the Far East to escape precision. As I stood on the bustling Bangkok pavement, drinking a long, iced glass of orange, I realized what it was that I loved about the East. No one really cared whether their quartz watches were three nanoseconds out of phase with some definitive atomic clock. The desire for exactitude which permeated through to every aspect of a Westerner's life seemed abhorrent here. Nobody really cared . . . except Quinlan. So, usually being at peace with myself, if not with the world, I was never fully prepared for the agitation with which Quinlan was constantly charged.

"You were supposed to meet me here at eight," he accused. I had forgotten our appointment.

He was right, and I wanted to apologize, but I found it difficult when I was under attack. Quinlan was a tall, morose character, an Australian freelance correspondent and adventurer, with some undefined purpose behind his wanderings. He had remained in the East after Vietnam, but unlike me he had little money, which seemed a constant source of bitterness to him. We tolerated each other's society simply because we were two Caucasians adrift in a sea of Asiatics. At home we would have avoided each other. I knew he envied me because of my resources and the fact that I could go home, or anywhere, whenever I wished. He was ten years older than I. I disliked him, and was afraid of him, because he seemed a little psychotic — brooding, intense and contemptuous of any form of authority. His thin face, usually carrying the sparse beginnings of a beard, held a pair of dark eyes that were never still. It was as if he expected to be assassinated at any moment. Despite being in awe of him, I respected him. He had been into Cambodia, at a time when visitors were more than discouraged, and had returned with his head still firmly on his shoulders. Two

Canadians who went with him were caught, by one side or the other, and tortured to death slowly, over a period of three days. Quinlan had witnessed the murder from a hiding place, unable to do anything to help. I found myself a rickety chair at the pavement café and sat down. Quinlan hovered for a few seconds and then joined me.

"Well, where were you?"

I forced my attention away from the passing faces, and focused on his belligerent expression.

"I'm sorry. I forgot our appointment. Naline did remind me earlier but . . ." I shrugged. "It's this place. There's so much going on." It had been my girl Naline who had introduced me to Quinlan. She had met him several days before me, at a party thrown by the Bangkok newspaper she worked for.

He stared at me for a full fifteen seconds, and for a moment or two I thought he was going to hit me. Then his thin face registered a look of resigned disgust and he sat down opposite. He put his feet on the edge of the table and tipped back in his chair.

"Christ," he said, explosively, looking straight into my eyes. It was one of those stares which, on the receiving end, was almost painful. I averted my own face.

"Trouble is," he said, "I need you. I need your . . . money."

"At least you're forthright about it. A little blunt and tactless perhaps . . ."

The money had been a gift — no, a bribe — from my father. He had intended that I use it to start a business in the United States, but when he died in London a year after my course at UCLA had ended, I skipped out of the States before my mother could contact me. They had been separated for ten years, and neither had wanted me around.

"Oh, you'll get it back. Tenfold," Quinlan said, suddenly leaning forward, his eyes only inches from mine. "I need a stake, Andy."

"What for?"

"I need you to finance an expedition. Christ, not a lot. Just some equipment and provisions. Well within your means, believe me. Trouble is, I need it soon, and. . . ."

"Collateral?" I queried.

His expression hardened again. For a few moments his

enthusiasm had driven out the bitterness.

"None. You'll have to trust me."

"I thought so. Where is it?"

"Where's what?" he seemed genuinely puzzled.

"Wherever it is you're going. I might want to come too."

He smiled, amused. "Doubt it. It's in Cambodia."

Cambodia. Immediately, the name conjured visions of green foliage folded in upon itself, many times. Shelves, layers of thick jungle. Underneath, dark, moody rivers, belly-sliding quiet as snakes through the undergrowth. Ruined temples, their stones torn apart by the vegetation. Then there were the man-made horrors. Skulls of massacred peasants piled into small hills. Horror stories manifested in the grotesque shapes of tortured bodies. Brains like dried paste upon rocks.

"I've been there," I said, stiffly.

"I mean alone. Not safely closeted inside a ring of soldiers."

"If it's my money you want, then I go with it," I replied. I meant it. Thailand was good for my soul but my body was deteriorating fast with all the abuse it received. It needed exercise and I needed excitement. Besides, Cambodia was relatively quiet now.

"And Naline," I added. "She goes too." (Naline had primed me before I left that morning. "Quin will be offering you a business deal," she had said. "It involves a journey. I'd like to come as well." Her forehead would crease into a tiny frown when she was being earnest, and her small Oriental mouth would purse into a bud. I found her irresistible.)

He smirked. "You've caught something there. It's a nasty infection."

"What?"

"Love. It's an illness, worse than typhoid. Okay, okay, don't get mad," he said, as I felt myself reddening with annoyance. "I guess I'll have to take you both. Can you climb? Mountains, I mean."

"You know I can. I told you . . . at the party the other night. The German Alps and Canadian Rockies . . . and in Cambodia," I added, after a pause. The insult regarding the army escort still smarted.

"Right. I remember . . . but you were stoned at the party. I wanted to be sure because there'll be no turning back once we've started. What about her? Naline?"

"She'll be okay. She's been climbing with me a couple of times."

"Do yourself a favour. Just lend me the money. If anything happens to either of you, I'm not turning back or stopping."

"We're coming," I said, determined.

Quinlan stared at me for a full minute, then said, "Right. I'll be here at nine tomorrow morning. Try and be here on time. It's not that difficult. All you have to do is look at your wrist."

I showed him the white mark where my watch had been, and he shook his head impatiently. "Well, for Christ's sake, ask somebody." Then he stood up and left, weaving his way between the stream of pedestrians. I sat and finished my drink before going to meet Naline. She was a beautiful Indo-Chinese girl, raised in Hong Kong. I met her on a climbing expedition in Cambodia about two years before coming to Thailand. She had been the official photographer for the Hong Kong sponsors. Quinlan was right about one thing — I was crazy about her.

I had to admit to being intrigued. Who can resist hints of buried treasure or the capture of some fabulous beast? Certainly not me. I am more susceptible than the next man to romantic visions and adventure. We began buying goods in accordance with lists he had already made out. There was food and hunting weapons, but the majority of purchases consisted of climbing equipment: ropes, pitons, hammers.

Lastly, and with the greatest difficulty, we bought the miners' helmets, complete with integral lamps and heavy backpacked batteries.

"Mines," I said eagerly, trying to remember what precious minerals came out of Cambodia. Gold? Silver? Quinlan merely smiled at me.

"No transmitter?" I asked later, I must confess a little anxiously.

"Who do you think's going to come and get us if we get into trouble? The U.N.?"

"What about if we get stuck half-way up a mountain?"

"Then we get ourselves down. Look, believe me, Andy." He always called me by my first name. I didn't even *know* his. "A radio would be no good to us. It'll only get us into trouble."

"Give our position away to terrorists, you mean?"

"Terrorists, or anyone. Who's a friend in the jungle? Some people I knew once sailed too close to the coast. They were on their way to Thailand, here, to buy teak for a new deck for their yacht. They were intercepted and fatally tortured by the *authorities*. Look, Andy, if you. . . ."

"I'm coming," I said, grimly.

"Suit yourself, but we do it my way."

The last purchase was a battered old Land Rover. That night Quinlan spent smoking hash, since, he said, he never got stoned when he needed his wits. I found a bottle of brandy somewhere and cuddled it all the way to Naline's place. Naline means Lotus Flower in Hindi, but to me she was more like some dark, mysterious orchid, with her black hair and fathomless eyes full of archaic secrets. I needed her more than I needed my brandy.

Next morning was as sultry as any other. The air in the room lay heavy and damp on my naked chest. I rose and showered, for all the good it would do me, and urged Naline to follow me through. We met Quinlan as prearranged, by Thieves' Market. We were half an hour late.

Quinlan was in the Land Rover's driving seat and gunning the engine impatiently. Naline and I joined him quickly and he smacked it into gear and tore out of the market place in a pique. I was getting used to Quinlan's tempers, though I guessed he always had them well under control despite what any onlookers may have thought. I believed much of it was an act. I suspected he enjoyed the role-playing, especially with an audience like myself and Naline.

The hard-dust roads seemed endless. Finally, several days out, we reached a point where we would have to go on foot. We abandoned the vehicle, hiding it by a waterfall, but we doubted it would still be there when we came back. I thought I had sweated out my soul in Bangkok. In the undergrowth the humidity was ten times worse. Within minutes there wasn't a dry patch on any of our jungle fatigues. I could hardly breathe, the air was so dense with moisture. It was as damp, dark and stifling as in the inside of a haystack.

The entangled foliage made the going difficult, and we took narrow paths wherever possible but kept clear of roads, crossing them quickly whenever we had to. If you've ever been in the jungle, you'll know that it's like being in a sauna crammed full of plants. Only the walls are made of tree trunks and the roof of thick, waxy leaves. The heavy air is alive with slow, dull-witted insects which fly into your mouth, ears and eyes, and all around you the disembodied calls of formless beasts follow your progress.

Quinlan spent most of his time poring over his compass and the maps: greasy-looking, weathered scraps of linen covered in sweat stains. At night we slept in a tight triangle. I say *slept* but I hardly closed my eyes. I have never been so afraid in my life: every tiny leaf rustling was man or carnivore on its way to my throat. There were too many unidentifiable sounds in the jungle. Strangely enough, Naline seemed the least concerned of the three of us. Perhaps she had an unfounded faith in our ability to protect ourselves. Or possibly she had a courage which shielded her outward appearance. Certainly she never seemed the least afraid. Once, she remarked to me, "You know, I always thought Quin would be at home in the jungle because he's so out of place in the city. But he doesn't fit in either environment, does he?"

"He's one of life's misfits, all right."

"And you," she said, her dark narrow eyes on my face, "in town you're different," which was a kind way of saying she recognized that, in town, I had my wallet. Her voice held a faint note of contempt.

We had been six days in the jungle when something happened which turned the journey into a nightmare for me. We were walking close to a hidden stream when I felt something snatch at my jungle fatigues. As I looked down, there was a sudden flurry in the long grass. I never saw what bit me.

Feverishly, I pulled up my trouser leg. My skin had been pierced just above the boot top.

Naline and Quinlan had walked on ahead, unaware of what had happened.

"Quin!"

He turned with a puzzled frown on his brow.

"What?" Then, "Why are you sitting down?"

I tried to keep my voice calm, but there was a tremor there which I could not quell.

"I think I've been bitten ... a snake."

"You think ...?"

"I have. It got me on the ankle."

He was very quick. Our first-aid kit had serum but there were many different kinds of snake. Quinlan cut my leg and made an effort to suck at the wound, but it was technically an amateurish operation. He was merely doing what he *thought* was the right thing to do. He gave up after a minute or two.

Naline injected me with a general serum and then stood back and observed me. There was no pain, but I was scared. I wanted to get up and run for my life. I fought the panic.

"You'll have to help me get back," I said, aware that my fright was making my heart race. They exchanged significant looks, and Quinlan said, "We can't go back now. We've come too far. The best thing to do is lie still. Moving will only ensure the poison reaches your heart and brain more quickly."

"You could carry me on a stretcher."

"No chance. We'd never make it in time — and the expedition would be a failure," he added, coldly.

"Fuck the expedition!" I shouted. "I could be dying." I climbed to my feet and tested my leg. Naline began taking photographs of me.

"Cut that out," I screamed at her. "I'm not a side show." She chewed her lip and frowned. "Sorry," she said, quietly. "It was a reflex action. Quin's right though, Andy. I couldn't carry you ... too heavy for me."

"We'll just have to hope for the best," said Quinlan, and that was the sum total of the psychological comfort I was going to get from either of my companions. For one whole day we remained where we were, procrastinating for no sensible reason. Maybe it was sympathy on their part, and dilatory manoeuvres with an acceptance of death, on mine. Nothing happened. I developed no feverish symptoms or pains in the chest, and finally we decided that the snake was nonpoisonous. We moved on at dawn, the second morning after. Quinlan remarked, when it was clear that I was going to be all right, that he had never understood the rationale behind the creation of creatures with a defensive weapon that, when used, still gave the victim adequate time to kill. I replied that perhaps the knowledge that it could be fatal was enough. What *I* had never understood, if these things were *meant* to fit within a pattern of order and not chaos, was why many of them were capable of overkill. There were creatures carrying enough poison to stop the heart of an elephant in places where the largest animal was the size of a dog.

Before we broke camp I noticed a thin red line running up from the teeth marks on my leg, following a vein. I said nothing to the others.

Three days later we reached a small clearing where Quinlan paused. "This is where Rice and Baker died," he said.

The Canadians.

"Christ!" I looked around me nervously.

Quinlan stood there a long time, just staring. I muttered something like, "Let's get going," and he turned on me.

"You know what happened here?" he cried.

"Keep your voice down," I urged. "Yes, I know. You told me." Naline was looking from one to the other of us, her eyes narrowed.

"What I didn't tell you was that while they had those two staked out over beds of bamboo knives, I had to belly-crawl to get the charts."

I was horrified. "You took them while they were dying?"

"There was no other way. I couldn't help them. The place was thick with bandits. It took me two nights to get up enough sweat to crawl out to them. What did you want me to do? I had to watch those two guys being roasted afterwards. They were my friends, for God's sake." His black lank hair hung over those restless eyes, and something was squeezing my windpipe, making my breath whistle softly. I turned away and busied myself with my pack until I had regained control of my emotions. When I turned around again, Naline had her hand on his arm. He was shaking violently. "You'll be all right, Quin," she said.

Later, he talked more rationally about his reasons for needing the maps and charts.

"Without them, we'd never find the place we're looking for," he said.

"What is this thing we're looking for?" asked Naline. "Come on, Quin, you can tell us now. We must be close."

Had it been I who asked, Quinlan would probably have ignored me. Instead he said, "Sure. You've got a right to know. Now." We were sitting round a small fire, risking the smell of woodsmoke reaching the nostrils of bandits. We weren't worried about anyone spotting the flames, since we were completely shrouded by a canopy of interlacing tree branches and surrounded by foliage: we were enclosed within a basket of jungle weave. Nearby a waterfall roared continuously. Naline called it a *stonewater-dragon*. It wasn't difficult to walk right into those hanging jaws with their silver teeth, in the density of the undergrowth. "Now we're on high ground, I'll tell you." His eyes seemed to glow with excitement. "We're looking for the fourth primary."

I looked at him, not in amazement, but in utter bewilderment.

"A new colour," he explained. "Only three primary pigment colours are known to man. It's possible this may be the fourth."

He was crazy. I should have realized all along that Quinlan was completely out of his mind. And was looking at *me*, as if *I* were the biggest dodo he had ever had the misfortune to pair up with.

"What's this colour like?" I asked, tentatively. My leg was hurting badly by this time. I had tried to clean it but the wound kept festering. It was not snake poison, but good old-fashioned septicaemia. All this for a madman.

"How the hell can I describe a colour you've never seen? All I can say is, it's not yellow, red or blue. I haven't even seen it myself — but it's there."

He launched into two or three scientific-sounding explanations which might account for a new colour, even improbable (I would have said impossible) theories for a new primary pigment involving half-wave lengths and mixtures of wave lengths, until I asked him to stop.

"I don't understand a word," I said, irritably. "For all we know, it could be supernatural effusion." I was trying to be sarcastic, but

Naline said, "That too, maybe." Quinlan smiled at me. So she was on his side? They were both of them insane, and I was stuck with them until he showed me the way back.   •

"What form is it in?" I said.

"Good question, but I don't know that either. I guess perhaps minerals," replied Quinlan.

I said, "What are you going to do with it?"

Naline smiled at Quinlan. "I can tell you that. Anything and everything. I can imagine the value of a new cosmetic for women. Or ornaments ... figurines. A new colour ... It'll be worth a fortune."

"What if it's in the form of a crystal," I said, quickly and stupidly. "You won't be able to mould it into shapes."

"Are you *kidding?*" Quinlan said. "If it's crystal, we're rich beyond measure. A rare crystal of a previously unknown colour. Hell!"

His eyes shone with lunacy. The *fourth primary*. Crazy. Crazy. After a few moments they both began laughing, first Naline, then Quinlan. Whatever this thing was, Quinlan cried, it would be marketable. Even a dead flower could be encased in plastic or fibre glass in order to retain its colour. They danced around the trees while oblivious of the danger we might be in, laughing themselves silly. Then they hugged and kissed each other, and me, in between fits of hysterics. I remember thinking at the time that she held on to Quinlan longer than necessary but then dismissed the thought. How long was necessary? Who was I, who hated timescales, to question the length of a hugging period? They were both intoxicated with pictures of our futures and I admit it was infectious. When the giggling had died, I calmly asked how Quinlan was so sure about the colour if he had never seen it.

"A Frenchman found it in the late fifties. He wrote a letter to a friend. The friend later emigrated to Canada and I met him in the sixties. We planned an expedition with another guy. You know how it ended."

"What did the letter say?" I asked.

"He wasn't *that* good a friend. I took his word for it that he knew what he was doing. All he told me was that the Frenchman had found a new colour and that it was in a marketable form."

"Did he have any special equipment with him?"

"He had a backpack he would never let me touch. Whatever he was after, the answer lay in that pack. The bandits got that. . . ."

"And the other Canadian?" I asked.

"He only knew as much as I did."

Naline said, "What happened to the Frenchman, Quin?"

"He caught something — a jungle fever — and died on a sampan that was taking him to Hong Kong. His personal effects we handed to a customs official. The letter was amongst them." Quinlan shrugged. "Anyway, we'll soon find out."

"The *fourth* primary," I said again, unnecessarily.

"Could be. Yes."

The foliage had been thick and knotted together, and when we had cleared it, I stood looking at the holes in the rock at our feet. Naline took some shots of them. Seeing the camera made me aware of my wound. It was not going to be easy with a bad leg. "I thought we were going to climb upwards?" I said. I was beginning to feel that I was being deceived at every turn. Potholing. We had to climb down, *underground*. I was afraid of being trapped, stuck in some crevice deep in the darkness of the earth. Above us, the mountains heaved, first in heavy green and then in darker colours. Leaden mists groped between the layers of trees, and in the hanging valley to the left the rock edge appeared, suddenly sharp against the sky. It was a scene transported from prehistory: its dull weight terrible on the back of the modern world. No people lived in this place.

"What if it rains while we're down there?"

"Then we'll probably drown. But it won't. The wet season is months away."

"Still. . . ." I could not help but feel terror, staring down at those three mouths of Hell. Psychologically, there is something very disturbing about going below the surface of the world. It was like entering the stomach of some great beast by crawling down its throat. At any second the jaws might snap shut, imprisoning me forever.

"Whatsamatter? Don't you like returning to the womb?" said Quinlan, smiling maliciously. I ignored him. It was not a womb, not to me. A womb is a safe, warm place where one can curl up and allow oblivion to creep over the soul.

"Which one do we go down?" asked Naline, hitching her pack high on her narrow shoulders. She was more ready than I was, but then by now I knew she was strangely attracted to Quinlan. Whether it was his enigmatic moodiness (which I'm sure she confused with a tortured soul) or the other side of him, the swashbuckling, carefree face which he showed us when he was not brooding on something, I had no idea. Anyway, what she found in him probably contrasted favourably with my simple, forthright personality. Like many people, she preferred a mysterious character to an open one. He was the deep one, and I the shallow. I was sure she wanted to plumb the depths of his soul, having dipped into mine and found it close to the surface.

Quinlan answered her question. "We go down the one on the left. The other two are blind windows."

I looked up. "Blind windows?"

"Windows in the rock that lead to a dead end. Nowhere. Like blind alleys. We'll encounter quite a few of them. That's why we need all these charts." I stared at the pieces of folded linen to which he was referring. I had looked at them while he had been asleep ... and could make nothing of them at the time.

"Just so long as you don't lose us down there," I remarked as casually as I could.

"No chance. This is my forté — potholing. Why'd you think the Canadians wanted me? For my good looks?"

I was suspicious. "How come you never told me?"

"There wasn't any need to. However, I know you've done a bit of mountain climbing. It's similar in some ways, totally different in others. At least you won't panic. You *won't* panic, will you?" His dark eyes searched my face.

"No."

"Good, because between us we've got to look after this little lady here."

Naline said, stiffly, "I'm capable of looking after myself," and turned away from us.

In such relationships, we prepared to descend into the guts of Cambodia. Out of the human dangers of the jungle and down into the elemental dangers of the subterranean. In search of what . . . a *colour?* We were mad, all of us. Me especially, since I recognized our insanity and still allowed myself to be swallowed. Would we even recognize our holy grail if ever we saw it? Could our eyes, our brains, register something of which no other human had any concept? Perhaps the dead Frenchman had had a particular kind of colour blindness which made a perfectly ordinary red, yellow, blue or derivative thereof, seem unique in a strange light? How did I know that the red which I could see was the same colour that Naline's brain registered? Or, more likely, perhaps either the Frenchman, the two Canadians or Quinlan was a schizoid, and the whole thing was a fantasy of one, or all of them? My head was spinning as I was lowered down, into the blackness, and my legs cycled in mild apprehension as I sought a foothold on the first of many ledges. Then my lamp began to pick out the rock walls of our pothole, smoothed by running water and glistening as the light swung back and forth. My leg jarred when I finally hit a shelf. I knew I was making a mistake but Quinlan had me cold. If I attempted to argue, he would just leave me behind. I did not know the way home, fool that I was. Soon we were edging through narrow crevices and scrambling over boulders. Sometimes dizziness overtook me but I rested for a few moments only. Quinlan was capable of abandoning me, if he knew I was sick.

We are in a place of perpetual night. Without our lamps there would be eternal darkness. I drove such thoughts out of my head and concentrated on the hand and footholds, while listening to the sound of distant water echoing in the sepulchral void which we were penetrating. Quinlan went first, constantly consulting his charts as we came to numerous forks in the tunnels. A blind window, he warned us again, could lead us to our deaths.

Of that, I had little doubt. We found one or two pits that appeared to be bottomless. I dropped stones and abandoned the place without ever hearing the final clatter. An uncanny deep silence, where there should be a noise, is the worst *sound* in the world. Things touched me in the darkness. Spiders, I thought. Perhaps lizards? The deeper we went, the wetter the rocks became. We rested frequently, and during those pauses I prayed that our lamps would hold out. It was hot too, and there was a musty, earthy smell like a freshly dug grave, which bothered my nostrils constantly. Once, Naline slipped into a side pocket and dangled, screaming, between us. After listening for so long to the silence, my ears were highly tuned, and the pitch of her cries drove needles into my brain. Quinlan pulled her up slowly and we comforted her until she had recovered her composure. We then continued along corridors of inner darknesses: tunnels untouched by the sun since their formation.

Suddenly, we began climbing.

"Quinlan!" I called, wincing afterwards at the railing echo. It seemed sacrilegious to break the cathedral stillness of the catacombs. Almost as if priests might converge upon me, from the shadows of hidden alcoves, and condemn my soul to the Devil for destroying their holy peace.

He either chose not to hear, or ignored me. We began to ascend a chimney, legs and back, and I had no energy for further talk. At the top was a cavern, with a low ceiling where stalactites and stalagmites, the fangs of the underworld, impeded our progress and we had to squeeze between them. Then more windows, presumably some of them blind, and on and on, upwards and along, but not *down* any more. We continued, with rests, for approximately eighteen hours.

Finally we came to a place where Quinlan suggested we sleep. He was highly excited for some reason, and when I asked why he would only say:

"The Canadian told me about this place. Night outside now. When day comes you'll understand. Feel anything? The breeze?"

He was right. I could. The soft brush of air against my cheek.

We slept. At first Naline had an arm around each of us, but I woke later to find that she was curled foetus-like against Quinlan. I was too feverish to be concerned, and, anyway, it looked too innocent to cause me jealousy: probably the vagaries resulting from a condition of half-sleep were responsible. I finally awoke to the sound of Naline saying softly, "Look, Quin, stars."

I followed the line of her arm, which pointed upwards, and saw what appeared to be the night sky. Something else had changed but I could not pin it down.

A more studied observation proved Naline wrong. They were not stars but distant cracks in the rock through which the daylight shone. There were hundreds, perhaps thousands of them. We appeared to be in some kind of enormous cavern, a hollow mountain, and the light from these fissures lit this inner world with much the same candle power as starlight on a moonless night. We could see, but very dimly. I could make out the shapes of rocks and, nearby, a vast underground lake. There were plants too, around our feet.

"We're *here*?" I asked.

"The Frenchman assessed it as six kilometres in radius and the daylight two kilometres away at its nearest point."

"What else did he say?" Naline questioned.

"There's life here. Animal life as well as vegetable. Listen. . . ."

We did so, and suddenly I mentioned what it was that had bothered me before. There was a faint but constant twittering sound, with an undercurrent of rustling. I looked at Quinlan. "Birds," I said. "On the ceiling. They must squeeze in through the cracks."

"Right. And bats. Maybe some of them live and die in here, without ever seeing the outside world. Could be there are fish in the lake too."

"Really?" said Naline, sounding surprised.

"Why not? Birds would bring in spawn on their legs. And perhaps a stream from the outside feeds this lake? Let's set up camp here. I think we should treat every move from now on with caution."

We were in a new world. A place of half-darkness shut away from ordinary life. The knowledge was exhilarating and yet a little terrifying. Should anything happen to us in here, we would get no help from anyone but ourselves.

"I suggest we conserve the batteries to the lamps," said Quinlan. "Our eyes will soon get used to this light. We should begin searching soon. I reckon we're looking for something living — a plant or a mollusc."

"A mollusc?" said Naline.

"Yes. Something like the banded murex found in the Med. A seashell the Romans used to crush for the purple dye in its stripes. . . ."

I wanted to know more about where we were and what was in here, but Quinlan would tell me nothing beyond the fact that we were in a cavern. "The Frenchman's notes just gave the dimensions — or his estimate of them. What the hell do you want? We're here now. From this point in we're on a voyage of discovery. Enjoy it."

"I'd like to know what was in the Canadian's backpack," I said.

Quinlan replied easily, "I don't give a toss what you'd like, pal, just so long as it doesn't bother me."

We sat down to eat some of the rations we had brought with us. I chewed on some dried fruit. When the meal was over I went apart from the other two to inspect my leg. It was ugly with pus and inflammation. I washed it and changed the dressing before rejoining them. Apart from the soreness, I was beginning to feel light-headed and faintly nauseous. I was almost certain that I had been bitten by a rat, not a snake as I first thought. The other two did not appear to be interested, now that I had not keeled over within a couple of days of being bitten. It may have been pure supposition, but I got the impression that from time to time they exchanged significant glances. What had happened while I slept? Had they whispered the time away to each other, exchanging secrets? Did Naline think I was so foolish as to believe that nothing had grown between them over the past few days? Perhaps they had already . . . ? My mind flash-fired with anger. I tried to concentrate on my surroundings, inspecting the lake and its environs. The light from the "stars" shone on the placid stillness of the water. As Quinlan had said, my eyes began rapidly to adjust to the gloom. Around the lake rose the humped shapes of its rocky shores. I wondered how the place was formed. A volcano? Or water erosion? My reverie was interrupted by a soft splashing sound.

"What was that?" I said, startled.

Suddenly I was alert. Quinlan often spoke of having an animal sixth sense, but I have never believed in vague superpowers, merely in a heightening of the existing five senses.

"What was what?" asked Quinlan.

"That noise."

Naline said, "Probably a bird, or fish, or something. Stop being so wet, Andy." She giggled at her own pun and the sound rippled out over the water. I was agitated for some reason.

"Be quiet, you stupid. . . ." I began, but stopped myself in time. Her laughter ceased abruptly and she said, "Yes, Andy?" Then she turned away. Quinlan was staring at me aggressively.

"Nothing. I'm sorry," I replied uncomfortably. "I'm getting . . . look, I think I'll explore for a bit. Can you flash one of the lamps every four minutes, so that I can find my way back?"

"Suit yourself," said Quinlan.

"Will you flash the lamp?"

He nodded curtly.

I stumbled away from them, my bravado rapidly dissipating with each step. Very soon I became aware of an intense feeling of loneliness, but nothing would induce me to turn round and go back to them. They were talking about me, I was sure, reaffirming their growing interest in each other. Well, to hell with them. Let them fuck each other. What did I care?

The trouble was, I cared a lot. Too much. I cared that I was losing Naline, and I cared that it was Quinlan, of all people, who was taking her away from me. What was it that impressed her? His erratic behaviour? His stupid hair cut? What? I could climb as well as he. I had more money. What did she want? Someone who mumbled in his cheeks like Brando?

I looked back. The torch flashed three times.

I stumbled over a soft patch between the rocks and switched on the torch. Moss, and some other kind of plant a little like saltwort, squelched beneath my feet. Perhaps this was where we would find the molluscs? Gingerly I turned over a stone in the soggy weed. A thin tentacled starfish slid out making me jump back, squeamishly. Shining my torch behind the patch of dark moss, I illuminated an area of more plant life, this time reed-like and brittle-looking.

A splash behind me made me spin. I was as stiff as a pole, my light searching the surface of the water. Then I found him. My breath caught in my throat and I almost screamed.

About twenty metres out was a naked man lying flat on his belly on what appeared to be a reed raft. He was paddling it with his arms, in an overarm swimming motion. I snapped off the lamp and stood there, shaking violently. Was it a man? Had he pinpointed my position? I began to hurry back towards the others as quietly as I could. My breath sounded abnormally loud, and my ridged climbing boots squealed on the hard surface. I slipped and stumbled once or twice, then stopped and crouched behind a tall rock, listening. All I could hear was my own blood pounding in my ears. I saw the lamp flashing ahead and began to make towards it, gratefully.

"Quinlan," I said breathlessly on reaching them. "There's someone here." I tried to explain what I had seen while they listened in silence. When I had finished my rather inarticulate account, Quinlan said, "There must be another way in. Show me where you saw him."

"Now?"

"Of course now. What's the matter?"

"Nothing," I said. Why should I give him the satisfaction of knowing I was uneasy . . . more than uneasy, paranoid. I led him back to the place where I had seen the boatman, Naline following, presumably because she did not relish the idea of staying alone. We were careful not to use our flashlights. As we neared the mossy patch, we could hear a low murmuring. I counted about seven of them standing, but at least two were kneeling, beside something white. It was not easy to judge how tall they were, especially in natural light, but I guessed not one of them was over four feet. They were all naked, but since they were huddled together, it was difficult to tell males from females. There was a body at their feet. I was trembling, both with excitement and fear, my attention absorbed completely by the people before me. Naline and Quinlan, too, were silent: just the soft sound of breathing near my head.

Suddenly the group on the moss lifted the supine body above their shoulders and carried it towards the rock wall at the back of the cavern. They soon disappeared from view.

"What shall we do?" I whispered.

"Wait," replied Quinlan. "They've gone into an opening — probably a subsidiary cavern."

We stood for about an hour, by which time my muscles were screaming and on the edge of a bout of cramp. Quinlan suddenly gripped my shoulder hard, and I saw the small group emerging from the shadows, one by one. It was too gloomy to get more than an oblique idea of their shape and build, but they definitely appeared to be humans. They each picked something off the ground at the water's edge, stepped into the shallows, and paddled off, out into the lake. Eventually, the last one had gone. Quinlan tapped my hand and we began making our way quietly towards the dark window, with Naline holding on to my belt.

Using our lamps, we entered the recess. As Quinlan had guessed, it was a smaller, subsidiary cavern about the size of a village church. I played the light around the walls and saw that shelves had been cut into the rock. There were bundles lying on the platforms and the air was thick with a foul odour. We inspected the nearest shelf. It held a corpse, the bones sticking through the dry flesh. There was very little meat left on it, and when Quinlan poked the abdomen with his finger, the taut brittle skin cracked open like a thin carapace. The next two hollows held only bones. Finally we came to a fresh one: presumably the creature that had just been laid to rest. *Creature*, because that word described it more accurately than the term *human*. Although the lips, nostrils and eyelids had been sewn up tightly, it was plainly the face of a monkey. A man's body: a monkey's face.

"Jesus," I heard Quinlan whisper.

There was a soft groan from Naline. We turned the lights on to her face. She had gone a deathly grey and she was backing towards the exit.

"*Hanuman*," she whispered.

Quinlan and I looked at each other in obvious incomprehension.

"*Hanuman*," she repeated. "A god!"

There were times when Naline seemed totally Westernized in her attitudes, but now she had retreated behind an Asiatic cultural screen and was inaccessible.

"This one's no god," grunted Quinlan. "Nor his friends and relations. They're primitives of some kind."

"Not animals though," I mused. "Tools . . . the single-man rafts. And one of the first signs of civilization is reverence for the dead."

I think there must have been a buzzing in all our minds when we left the burial chamber a few minutes later. There was certainly one in mine. None of us spoke about it, but I think we all realized we had found a new race of men. Subhumans, perhaps, but very close to us. It was not something we *could* put into words yet: it was too important to try to frame it orally. We had, each of us, to allow our own turbulent feelings to evolve into some form of rational acceptance of the unacceptable. Naline was clearly very shaken. Somewhere in her culture there was a mythological creature very like the one we had just seen. I wondered how *I* would feel if our friend had had cloven hoofs, horns and a little pointed head. He had been startling enough to me. To her, he was the manifestation of a familiar childhood dream, perhaps a nightmare. Late that night we spoke of it again and Naline told us the story of *Hanuman*.

"He was the son of the wind-god, *Vayu*, and one legend says his mother was a monkey. Another that he mistake the sun for golden fruit and sprang three thousand miles into the air to reach it. The sky-god, *Indra*, was afraid and broke his jaw giving him ape-like chin."

"There's more to it than that," I said. "You accepted the idea too readily."

"Yes." She hung her head. "*Hanuman's* Chinese counterpart, *Monkey*, was buried under a mountain by *Buddha*. This was punishment meted to *Monkey* for drinking jade juice and ruby extract, so that his body became as hard as a diamond and invulnerable. We are . . . under this mountain. I was afraid at first but that was silly. I'm all right now."

"Well, what do we do about these . . . people?" I asked. "Do we just ignore them, or study them, continue searching for our lost colour? What?"

"Maybe observe them to a degree," Quinlan said. "But we're not anthropologists. We don't know what's important. When we get out, then I can come back with a trained team."

"Should you do that?" I said.

Naline looked at me hard.

"Why not?" she countered.

"You know what will happen. They'll be installing soft-drink machines in here within a year."

"You mean we should leave them in peace? Like good little conservationists?" sneered Quinlan.

I replied, "If we get what we came for, why should we need to trouble these people?"

"Fame," he said, bluntly.

"If we find a new colour, we *will* be famous. Perhaps the prestige of discovering a lost tribe would be greater, but our fortunes and all that goes with it will be assured."

"And if we don't find it?" Naline asked.

I was adamant. "The Frenchman found it. We'll find it. Let's leave these people alone."

I sensed, rather than saw, Quinlan nod at Naline. I knew him well and what his reaction to conservation would be. I was rich, he was poor, he would say. People with money could afford to be philanthropic; could afford to have integrity. Those without it were entitled to exploit whatever they were able, after which they too could develop morals. I had heard the speech and did not want a repeat.

"Get stuffed," he said, finally, under his breath. "I'll do what I think's right, from *my* point of view."

"Well, think *hard* about it, Quin," I said. "I'm tired. I'm going to hit the sack. Are you coming, Naline?" My head was spinning and I needed sleep.

Her voice was small in the darkness. "I'll stay up for a bit. I want to talk to Quin. You go ahead though."

Anger flooded through me. Having said I wanted to bed down, I could hardly stay without seeming childish. I crawled into my sleeping bag, a few yards away, and fell into a deep sleep with their mumbled conversation, just too low to understand, gently fanning my annoyance. Conspiracy. I could not get rid of a Shakespearean word that persistently picked at my brain. *Hugger-mugger*. They were *Hugger-mugger*. Later, I heard them creep away. I knew where they were going and what they were going to do. Naline would have one of her cameras with her. They were going to the tombs.

We spent the next few starlit days searching our immediate

environment. Occasionally we came across one or more of the monkey-people but they would never let us get close to them. They drifted in and out of sight like distant phantoms reluctant to allow direct contact. As far as I was concerned, the policy was mutual. I had no wish to disturb or interrupt the rhythm of this underground world in any way, except perhaps in the course of locating the mystical, perhaps imaginary, new colour. In Naline's case, I was sure that the desire for fame at any price was just a matter of following Quinlan's footsteps. She had clearly been shaken by their appearance, and cultural fears ran deep, but she was also infatuated with Quinlan. I observed her narrow brown eyes as she, in turn, studied him. He was often belligerent towards me and at such times she retreated behind one of her Asiatic masks. There was no doubt that her loyalties had undergone a change, and my physical (and mental) condition made me react with bouts of sullen jealousy, and pushed her further towards him. She was fascinated by him in the way that someone is intrigued by a creative artist with dark moods. She wanted to *understand* him, perhaps.

They were spending their nights together now. Nothing was said, by any of us, but a wall had gone up. I took my sleeping bag and settled well away from them, occasionally even eating on my own. To his credit he allowed no overt demonstration of affection, but that only made the situation bearable, not acceptable. I was still fond of her, but I hated him. Sometimes I almost choked on exchanging the merest civilities with him. Mostly, I had to get out on my own and leave them to each other's company.

Success eluded us. We found many unusual shades, but all had the familiar base tinge of the three primary colours. Our supplies began to run low and we started fishing the lake for extra food, pulling in pale and often translucent specimens. Naline was constantly photographing the scenery, and us, but could never entice the monkey-men near enough. I did not tell her that ironically it was probably the continual flash of her camera that kept them away. It was a strange feeling, sitting alone in a half-lit world where the natural sounds of birds and animals threw muted echoes into dark corners. It all seemed so unreal. It *was* unreal. Occasionally I would hear the distant splash of small hands propelling rafts across the still surface of the lake. (We had still not found their community home, though to be truthful we stayed clear of subsidiary caverns that looked as if they might be occupied. We had no idea of their numbers and they might have turned hostile.)

I was still very sick. My body temperature was constantly high. The pain had increased in intensity. I knew, also, that blood poisoning could be fatal, and this worried me unceasingly. Once or twice I tried to explain my predicament to the other two but they kept repeating, "Soon. We'll go home soon. Give it another day." And the days came in and went out.

Suddenly a wave of resentment washed over me one morning. A cruel trick entered my mind through the dizzy wash of thoughts, and without pausing to consider, I made my way to where I knew I would find the other two.

"Quinlan," I called, scrambling up towards them. "Quickly, I think I've found something." I introduced as much excitement into my voice as I could muster. He jumped to his feet. "What? What's the matter?" He looked startled. Naline sat up, groping for her shirt, hiding her breasts with her hands. A silly gesture, since I had seen her naked many times before.

"I've found something. Quickly." I set off at a steady pace, stepping around rock stacks and pillars. Quinlan followed, though less actively. I led him a quarter of a mile and pointed upwards to a ledge I had climbed to on my own, the previous day. "There!" I started to find the handholds and pull myself up. I heard him mutter something and then sensed he was following.

The climb was difficult and dangerous in my rapidly deteriorating condition, but it had a reward at the other end which was worth the pain.

It took quite a while to reach the rock shelf. We were both panting for breath as we heaved ourselves up over the hanging lip. We were about sixty feet from the bottom, and I knew that the climb down would be even more strenuous.

I sat against the face, recovering while Quinlan looked frantically around him. "Where?" he said. I remained silent and eventually he saw a clump of fungi on a damp area near the edge.

"Fungus?" he said, switching on his lamp. He stepped eagerly towards it and broke a piece off to study it under the artificial light. After a few minutes he shone the light on my face. I could not keep from smiling.

"You *bastard*," he swore. "It's bloody *purple*. Don't you know . . . yeah, yeah, you know, you shit." He threw the fungus at me hard, and it splattered painfully on the side of my head. Then he seemed to go berserk, screaming at me in a high, womanish voice and flinging great lumps of the stuff at my head. I put my hands over my face, laughing into my palms as the fungi struck the rock wall behind, and occasionally hit me. Then something happened. I think he slipped on a damp patch. I heard the note in his voice change and looked up to see he was no longer standing there.

"Andy!" The tone was urgent, desperate. Then I saw his hand gripping the edge, the knuckles white with the effort of holding on.

"Andy! God, please . . ."

I reached out, hesitating only for a split second, then he was gone, without a sound. I heard his body hit the bottom with a loud crack. His head. Then Naline's screams came up to me. After a long while they changed to sobs, and slowly I began to descend.

She was looking out across the water when I finally reached the bottom. We sat for an hour, just staring at the body, when small sounds drifted to us over the lake. They were coming to us now, about thirty of them, on their small rafts, close together for reassurance. When they reached the shore, they came forward as a group, touching each other repeatedly. Ignoring Naline and myself, they clustered around the body, moaning softly and making slight, indefinite gestures. Then some of them lifted the body on to their shoulders and began to move off.

"Wait!" I called, but only one, a male, took any heed. He came back and looked up at me, curiously. I shone a light into his monkey face. Then I began laughing again — the same kind of laughter that had overwhelmed me on the ledge — and he ran off in fright. But I found it impossible to control myself. It was so ironic. So *damned* unfair. Eventually I was aware that Naline was pounding me with her small fists, sobbing, "Stop it. Stop it.

Stop it." And I choked on the sound and finally subsided into my own tears of grief and frustration. Perhaps we were crying for different reasons, I don't know. I believe we were.

"He was *Hanuman*, your god-monkey," I said at last. "Why didn't he show us before?"

"You're not sane any more," she said. "This place has turned your brain. Keep away from me. I don't want you near me. You could have saved Quin. You let him die, you bastard."

"I tried to . . . I reached out, but he was gone before my hand could touch him. It's you who is insane, not me. I reached out. . . ."

"Too slow, Andy. You were too slow."

Perhaps she was right? Maybe I was mad? I did not care any more. I had seen *him. Monkey.* There were dozens, females too. Under the mountain, placed on them by *Buddha*, they had bred since the time Earth belonged to the gods, since they walked abroad and among mortals. "*HANUMAN*," I called, the sound echoing over and over.

"They're just people," said Naline quietly. "Just ordinary people."

Then I told her. The eyes. The colour was in their eyes. I knew now what had been in the Canadian's pack. A net, tranquilizer darts, something to catch a man. The Frenchman had found a lost tribe with unique face and eyes. The Canadian wanted to take one back to civilization. Quinlan had not been that ambitious. A new colour and some photographs of monkey people would have satisfied him. *Photographs!* That night I stole Naline's cameras and threw them into the lake. When she found out, she screamed abuse at me and said she was going to leave me to die. I believed her.

Over the following few days my physical condition deteriorated even further. The fever would not leave me, and I stumbled around with heavy limbs, aware of the thickening of my speech but unable to control it. Thoughts moved in and out of my aching brain with viscous consistency. My dreams became tangible, organic scenes that I carried in my head, awake or asleep. Around the wound left by the bite, the skin had turned a blackish-yellow and smelled.

Naline only spoke to me when she had to and studiously
avoided my eyes. She gathered together our possessions and
prepared to leave. Then another of the monkey-people died, and
after we had witnessed the body being carried into the tomb,
Naline said to me, "We could take him with us." It took a little
while for her remark to permeate to my reason.

"I . . . we could never carry him. Remember all those difficult
parts . . . couldn't climb out carrying a body. Too sick."

"We *have* to take *proof*," she said fiercely. "Otherwise Quin died
for nothing. The people outside will want us to show them proof
of the monkey-people's existence." Her voice became hard. "I
won't help you, unless you help me."

"Couldn't do it," I said, my head buzzing softly.

"You weak bastard. You always were weak."

"Wait. Wait. Got an idea. Look, we'll take the monkey-man's
head. I'll get it and we can wrap it in a wet cloth. Okay?" I said it,
though the thought of decapitating a corpse filled me with
distaste.

She seemed mollified. "Yes. The eyes. We must show them the
eyes . . . and face. Do it, Andy. We'll be famous. Quin too. It'll
make all this worthwhile, won't it?"

"I don't know," I said. "I suppose so." She was too strong for
me now. The pressure of her demands was too powerful to
resist. I took a machete, and when there were no monkey-people
around the tomb, I entered and found the shelf with the body.
Then, overcoming the natural revulsion that welled up to
collect in my throat, I hacked the head free from the corpse.
Outside the burial cavern, I wrapped the head in cloth soaked
in the lake. I had given Naline the idea that this would help
preserve it longer. Winding the strips around tightly, I knotted
them several times. When I had finished it, it looked like any
one of the innocuous bundles we carried in our backpacks. I left
a flap of cloth open at the grisly end of the neck and showed it to
Naline.

She winced at the sight of the raw flesh, then nodded dumbly.
I completed the wrapping, put the head in her haversack, and
then collapsed exhausted, to fall asleep.

During sleep I relived the severing of the head. I heard again
the short, sharp, "Uhh! Uhh! Uhh!" of breath as I chopped

through the spinal cord. The sawing of rubbery tendons. Thank God, the eyelids had been sewn. Although I carried out the actual act in the dark, I would have *felt* those eyes on mine, compelling, accusing.

Naline has taken with her all Quinlan's charts of the underground passages. Whether or not she is able to decipher them, I don't know. I hope she makes it, even though she has abandoned me. I guessed she would. When she went, I don't know.

My illness makes it difficult to think straight.

I am trapped, held captive by a network of blind windows. A man in a maze. There is only one way through them and many, many false trails. A single blind window might lead me astray for hours, into several more of its kind, until I am hopelessly lost. And these strange monkey-people. They sit around me, in a circle, their small wrinkled faces illuminated by the light from the lamp. As long as I sit quietly, they are not frightened. While I write this account, I can feel their breath on me. And their eyes, caught wide and fast in their fascination with the lamp, hold the colour for which we have searched for so long. How can I describe it to you, this new colour? I can't. I can see it, vivid in the light. It burns its hue into my retina. (An iris! Would we ever have thought of deliberately looking there?) Yet I cannot convey even an inkling of what it means to me. A ring of earnest faces, ancient monkey faces stamped with monkey wisdom, set with gems of a unique colour.

Tomorrow I shall attempt the climb to one of those fissures high above in the hope that it will be large enough to crawl through. I am weak with sickness, and the rock face is virtually sheer, but I am full of optimism. I will make it. Even if I don't, a fall is better than a wasting death. Quinlan went that way. Then they could have me, these clownish creatures. Death is an event in their dull lives: an entertainment. They danced and crooned over Quinlan's body for hours. No doubt they would do the same with mine: the light is in those eager eyes. An event!

They are waiting for the event!

Forgive me for saying I want to cheat them of the pleasure.

I wronged Naline, even at the last, but how could I betray those vulnerable creatures to mankind? Naline wanted to be close to Quinlan: well, she has him with her now, part of him at least. She has his head.

LORD OF THE DANCE

"One should try everything once, except incest and folk dancing."

M. Bax

I was a little annoyed with Denys. Spring Bank Holiday is never the best of times to be on the road, and she could have forewarned me of the festival by telephone. People blocked Thaxted's streets for as far as I could see, and in the distance colourful figures bobbed ribboned straw hats above the heads of the crowd. There was the sound of accordion music mingling with the note of the car engine. I glanced at the dash — the motor was beginning to overheat. Looking round, I saw a stone church wall that was indented and decided to park the Lancia there and return for it at a later time — when the crowds had thinned. It was late afternoon and hot. Hopefully they would not last long into the evening.

Denys was to meet me at The Argus, a presumptuous inn that called itself a hotel. She had started out by train a day ahead of me on our annual tour of Essex. As I moved through the crowds, I saw that the straw boaters belonged to a group of English folk dancers and that there were many more such groups standing by, awaiting their turn to entertain the watchers. They were dressed similarly in multi-coloured waistcoats, ribbons fluttering from elbows and shinpads of bells. I noticed from the coaches that they came from various parts of the country — even from as far north as York. Some held sticks in their hands, others swords, and, more commonly, the white handkerchiefs associated with Morris dancers.

I found a cool side street free of icecream lickers and over-dressed adults, and left them to the sound of clacking staves as six dancers weaved their way through a traditional number, jingling their leg bells and hopping in a clearly effeminate manner to the accompanying music. The street closed in around me as I walked over its shadowed cobbles. There were timber-framed overhanging houses interspersed with rows of dormered, gabled and colour-washed cottages throughout Thaxted. The place had that comfortable, solid feeling of age. I loved to visit it, more especially since to reach it one had to drive through the similar market towns of Cutlers Green and Saffron Walden. Thaxted, however, had a special significance for me.

It was not that I was overfond of 14th Century buildings but that the place was peppered with antique shops. I was a London market dealer, and my livelihood depended upon old ladies clearing their attics and small town dealers trading for less than city values. This particular weekend I had located an item I had been seeking for some time. There was a potential buyer on-hook requesting immediate purchase — a rich Arab apparently, and it was one of those rare, succulent name-any-price transactions.

To enter the Tudor-style Argus Hotel, I had to rejoin the main street once again, having circumnavigated the holiday-makers for a good part of the journey from the car. Humanity at its most ugly pressed against the pink walls and inset windows of the hotel. They were out in force: the trouser suspenders, the cardigans draped over shoulders, the chocolate smears around the mouths. There was even a street photographer, with a cheap Polaroid camera and a monkey, touting for business on the fringes of the mob. I hated them, not because they were a *crowd* but because they were a loose-jawed *circus-mob*, and of course they were not looking for Sheffield plate or solid silver antiques. Weddings and christenings I adored because people bought antiques as gifts for such occasions. Funeral crowds I could tolerate — a death might lead to the unearthing and sale of family heirlooms. Circus crowds however were detestable, useless gatherings. The monkey hopped on to a child's shoulder, and the Polaroid came up instantly to the wearer's eye. I left them with a feeling of revulsion.

Denys was in the bar. I stopped to admire her from behind. Her blonde plaits — a recent acquisition — appeared to be tangible echoes of the corn dollies pinned to the dark beams above her head. She saw me in the mirror over the bar and smiled without turning round.

"A pint of bitter," she ordered from the barman, then to me: "You took your time. Trouble with the car?"

I sat upon the stool next to her, complaining. "You know damn well why I'm late. The populace is out on the streets."

"The Morris dancing — actually, I'd forgotten. You know I wouldn't do this on purpose. It can be quite fun, you know, if you allow it to be."

Her softly spoken admonishment was enough to melt any feelings of annoyance that I had carefully nursed from the moment of my arrival at Thaxted. They had to a certain extent been contrived in any case. I smiled with her.

"You're right. And the . . ."

"Yes. It's still there. I'll take you when you've fortified yourself with the local ale."

She sensed my impatience and added. "It'll *still* be there. I asked him to hold it with a five-pound note. Don't worry."

I tried to relax as the beer was pushed towards me and from the high bar stool looked out through the window over the heads of the people outside. A new set of Morris dancers was mincing in festive delight, brandishing double-handed swords, forming arches with them and tripping beneath with what I had to admit was skilful footwork. It just did not entertain me as it seemed to do others. All I saw was a bunch of blue-ribboned farmer's boys in sissy clothes acting out a silly fertility rite — albeit traditional. I sighed.

"They're forming the nut with the swords now," said Denys.

The dancers had locked all the blades together to form a pentangle. One man held it aloft.

"You're a nut," I replied and received the expected rap on the knuckles.

I stared sourly at the scene outside. I had always viewed men who enjoyed nonprofit-making hobbies with suspicion. They threw themselves into their chosen pastime with an energy I believed was wasted. That was not the whole story though. It was not them, but me that was the trouble. I had once considered taking flying lessons until I realized one had to make a ritual of the procedures. A religion. Actually *flying* the aircraft was a minor side-issue. What really counted were the numerous checks and re-checks on the serviceability of the machine; the correct completion of flight plans; the exact order of the instrument check; the knowledge of meteorology, navigation and radio communications. . . . Eventually I realized that taking up flying as a hobby was a full-time job. You had to eat, drink and sleep *flying*.

There was nothing on this earth I liked enough to throw myself into so completely as that. Nothing that did not pay.

"Shall we go now?" Denys was on her feet. I admired her tall, upright body as she moved towards the door. Our affair was past tense and it had not altogether been a success. Perhaps if one of us had billed the other for the service, it might have been different? I am, I suppose, a natural cynic. Still, for some reason we made the work an excuse to stay together. She remained my partner in business, if not in bed. Denys dealt with the art and I with the age.

We went out on to the packed pavements. Denys led me through sightseers and past grim, sweating dancers to the end of the main street. On the corner, opposite the church but on the far side from where I had left my car, was a black-framed antique shop. A bell tinkled as we entered. A few moments later a small faded man of indeterminate middle age came gliding from the dark cloisters at the rear. He saw Denys and smiled.

"The astrolabe?" he said, but there was no need to reply. From a drawer behind his desk he took an object the size of a small saucer. I could see from the way he handled it that it was heavy. It was swathed in tissue which he unwrapped slowly. I stared through his thin hair at the skull as he bent his head over his task.

He placed the astrolabe in my hand.

When one usually talks of a "sixth sense", it is more often than not with a primitive warning of imminent danger in mind. An instinct. The legendary detective has a sixth sense which urges him to turn at the point when the villain's club is descending from behind. I have such a sense, but it is not in the form of a mental telemetry device — it is a talent most useful to my profession. *I can sense age.* Moreover, it appears to have a rejuvenating effect on me, as if my own years flow into the object, ageing it further and leaving me in hidden youth.

It was this strangeness about myself which attracted me to Thaxted. There were others like me, somewhere in the town. I could sense their presence. I had the idea that there was a colony of people like me that had collected in the area, possibly over a number of years. It was not something I could speak to others about, although I had almost blurted my secret to Denys once when she showed me a poem of which she was fond. The poem was almost like a sign telling me that I was not alone in the world. The last four lines were particularly interesting. They read:

> *The blast again, ho, ho, the blast!*
> *I go to a mansion that shall outlast;*
> *And the stoled priest who steps before*
> *Shall turn and welcome me at the door.*

It concerned the funeral of a wizard, and I knew I had something of the magician in me. I interpreted the lines to mean that people like myself had a special afterlife, where we would all meet and know one another — know ourselves for what we were.

The astrolabe was old, very old. My palm held centuries of secrets. I could feel the darkness and weight of many wars and long journeys. Moreover, and more practically, it was manufactured of bronze. The instrument consisted of two circular rings arranged as in an ancillary sphere. The centre plate was decorated with star patterns and planets, and there were several moving parts known as the horse, mater, rete and alidade. An astrolabe is the forerunner of a sextant and was originally used to measure the altitude of a heavenly body. It was developed in Ancient Greece but was, in the 15th Century, adopted by navigators for determining latitude. The "sighter" looks along a pointer pivoted across a vertical disc marked off in degrees of a circle. Moslems use them to determine *gibla* — the direction to face in prayer. There is a story that Herod sent an expert navigator after the Magi, but that while the agent of the king was taking a sighting with the astrolabe, a star suddenly exploded into brilliance and blinded him.

It was a beautiful object and, I guessed, pre-Christ. Egyptian or Greek. Or possibly Phoenician. I shrugged my shoulders unenthusiastically.

"It's not the type I was looking for but I can probably find a client. How does a hundred and fifty suit you?"

He relieved me of the object, temporarily, and the haggling began and finally settled at £250. I was happy. My client had promised a great deal more for such an item.

We left the dealer and set about fighting our way back to the hotel. In the centre of Thaxted is the guildhall, a 15th Century building of timber-shorn wattle-and-daub. The crowd had thickened, and after one or two attempts to work our way through Denys said, "Let's wander around the hall for half an hour. They *must* be going home soon."

I agreed. The guildhall was now a museum. Perhaps I would learn something about the townspeople there? We paid a small sum at the door and climbed a cool, wooden stairway to sanity above.

However, even in the small museum we were unable to escape completely the influence of the folk dancers in the street below. Anticipating an expansive interest in Thaxted's spring festival, the museum authority had arranged a display of costumes and accoutrements relating to Morris dancing. There were also photographs and several paintings of past dancers and their moments of glory. Some of the faded plates had been taken in the late eighteen-hundreds. The paintings went further back. Morris dancing apparently had its origins in pre-Christian Saxon England. In those times (I read) the dance consisted of six men, one of whom wore girl's clothing. There was usually a "fool" that struck the dancers — and spectators — with an inflated pig's bladder tied to a stick.

Not much had changed since the early days except that the male "lady" no longer appeared in the dance and, of course, the intention of the dance had become somewhat diverted. Fertility was not foremost of the participants' concerns, but entertainment.

"Interested?" asked Denys.

"Funnily enough, I am," I said. "These things have a way of reaching out and grabbing your attention."

I moved around the room and finally came upon a large painting hanging over an open fireplace. The picture was heavily lacquered, which gave it a dark, brooding atmosphere, and the paint beneath the varnish had cracked into an intricate, crazy mosaic. Close to, the figures were lost in the intermingling dull brown background and surface shine. Stepping back, I could vaguely make out six figures dressed in monkish garb and wearing reindeer horns. A seventh person stood apart from the rest. He was playing a fiddle. It was a faintly sinister scene, and I wondered why this should be so: why it disturbed me.

"Is this the Abbots Bromley Horn Dance?" I asked Denys, for although I had heard of the dance, she was much better informed than I on such matters.

She came and stood by me, studying the picture for a moment.

"No, I don't think so. The Bromley dancers wear Tudor dress and their horns haven't left the parish since the Anglo-Saxon period. Abbots Bromley is in Staffordshire," she explained. "Not Essex. Also it's to commemorate the granting of hunting rights in Needwood Forest and isn't performed until September."

Even I was surprised at the glibness of her reply, and she cocked her head to a corner of the room, confessing:

"I just read it all over there. You can see by the picture that this one was performed in Thaxted. That's the guildhall behind them."

I stared harder and realized she was right. It was Thaxted. Was this dance going to take place today? If so I wanted to see it. There was a fine quality of age about the picture that aroused my curiosity, and despite the numerous warning notices I touched the canvas. The effect was startling and I withdrew my hand quickly. It was as if my whole body had received a charge of undiluted malevolence.

"Naughty," said Denys, referring to my trespass.

"God, this one is very. . . ." I stumbled over the word.

"Old?"

"Not just old — something else." A trace of evil? It must have been apparent in my tone because Denys gave a short, nervous laugh.

"Now you're trying to frighten me. Come on, let's go and have a drink. Out in a pub garden preferably, where there's a bit of sunshine and light. . . ."

"Coward," I replied, but though I tried for banter, there was a tremor to my voice. I continued to study the painting, tried to capture one of the faces of the dancers in my mind, but either the light was too poor or the shades too dense. I could only make out individual features, such as a nose, or a cheek, or a set of ringed eyes, but not one of the portraits was clear enough to distinguish a full face. They were clouded features: not deliberately screened by hoods or limbs but obscured by hazy shadows. If I moved my line of sight, the shadows appeared to move with me. Thwarting my intention. The only unusualness about them was a silvery sheen under the eyes and on the nostril ducts. A whiteness where one normally found dark shadow. By moving my angle of sight I managed to pick out these individual characteristics. Of the seven figures, two were full and both had this peculiarity.

I followed Denys down the stairway, but before I had left the painting, something had attracted my attention. There had been a small, oval title plate which I had previously missed, possibly due to the fact that it blended with the heavy gilt frame.

The plate had read: *Danse Macabre*. The dance of death. Beneath that, a date: *1603*.

Societies and cultures throughout history have used the power of the dance for many reasons. More than just a form of expression, it is also a heavy intoxicating agent and has been employed as such for war, love, mysticism, magic, illness and death. Polynesians say hello and goodbye with a dance. Modern youth uses the dance to express contempt and rebellion. As a drug it can be as potent as heroin and the addict more manipulative. A dance might be the result of methodical calculations, or it might arise suddenly from obscure and mysterious origins to meet a situation such as the defeated Sioux's *Ghost Dance*.

My knowledge of dances was broadbased, not specific. I knew little about the *danse macabre* and I connected it loosely with visions of jigging skeletons. I mentioned it to Denys as I caught up with her.

"It has psychopathological connotations," she said at once.

"What?" I blinked rapidly.

She stared at me as if I were a simpleton.

"It's pathogenic. You can even kill people with it, providing the beliefs are deep-rooted enough — or so I understand," she added hastily as she saw the expression I was forming.

"Let's get a programme," I suggested.

We went out into the sunlight, and there the nefarious atmosphere of the museum left me. It was difficult to retain a mood of black magic with lighthearted holiday-makers elbowing my ribs.

There was a Horn Dance on the programme, scheduled for midnight. We could probably see it from the windows of The Argus, since most of the people would have gone home by that time.

I put my arm around Denys to steer her through the crowd, and the contact brought with it a wave of nostalgia. I was still very fond of her but had foolishly allowed her to slip away from me. I now regretted that immersion in work which had been responsible for my neglect of our love affair. A couple of younger men had come and gone since then, and I was too afraid of rejection to try again.

The astrolabe banged heavily against my hip as I walked. I reflected that the instrument could have belonged to one of those dancers in the picture. It was of a similar age. I dismissed it as too much of a coincidence.

Over dinner, later in the evening, Denys said to me, "This gift you have for judging age in objects — is it . . . real?"

"Don't worry," I replied frivolously. "It doesn't work on people." Then, seeing she was serious, I added, "Depends what you mean by *real*. It's only a feeling, you know — not something I could put a name to."

"No, you misunderstand me. I mean, you don't put it on — for effect? To give yourself a touch of mystique?"

I was a little offended. "Certainly not. You've seen it work in the past. I've usually been fairly accurate, haven't I?"

"Yes, but that could be luck. A good guess. Or perhaps your knowledge of the artifacts is more extensive than you prefer to reveal."

"I wouldn't do that with you. Possibly with a client or another dealer, but not with you. No, if you want me to take a stab at a phrase, I'd call it depth of perception. Everyone can perceive age to a certain degree — my gift, as you call it, is intrinsic, believe me. It's just more intense than that of others. Why?"

She looked at me thoughtfully. "I didn't want you to keep fooling me — if that's what you were doing. Now I'm sorry I mistrusted you."

I tried to look hurt but changed the subject.

"I like your dress," I said. "Is it new?"

She seemed grateful that I had let her off the hook and said, "Yes," at the same time adjusting the bodice a little.

The dress was low-cut and exposed a spray of those freckles which had fascinated me for as long as I had known her. She saw me staring.

"You don't think it's too revealing?" she asked with a crestfallen look.

I shook my head. "Not at all. It shows enough of you to whet the appetite of the other males in the room ... Don't be offended," I added hastily, "it's just a way of saying you're beautiful."

"Am I?" she smiled, warmly.

I was mumbling something inaudible to her when there was a stir of excitement around the windows. Other diners were looking out at the dancing, which was still in progress although the crowds had thinned until only a narrow ribbon of onlookers remained. Most of these would be tourists, gently ejected from the closing public houses a few moments before. They stood in knots under the cones of light beneath the street lamps, eating pies or finishing the remains of a pint of beer. They sounded far more cheery than I felt, and I excused myself, saying I was going to get an early bed. Denys looked a little disappointed but nodded and rose. I took her to her room, pecked her cheek and wished her good-night.

Once in my own room, which was on the first floor, I undressed and lay on my bed, hoping to fall asleep quickly. However, the room faced the street, and the accordion music proved difficult to keep out of my head. It demanded my attention. For a short time however, I must have dozed.

I awoke abruptly to a stillness which disturbed me, and I realized after a moment that the silence must have triggered my state of awareness. The accordion music had stopped. But then something began to take its place, a different kind of music. It was no longer a bouncing, tripping time but a slow, intricate melody that was not melodious. A pibroch, spontaneous and distantly melancholy. A dirge played, if I was not mistaken, on a fiddle.

I went up to the leaded window and looked down. There was only a small handful of onlookers left outside, one of them being a street photographer with his monkey sitting on his shoulder. He was preparing to take a flash of the horn dancers. The *danse macabre!* I had forgotten about it until that moment.

There were nine dancers, an incorrect number for a Morris dance, dressed in monks' habits and carrying short poles topped with antlers. Two more than the picture in the guildhall had shown. They held the staves in front of their faces so that the horns appeared to spring from their foreheads. Shadows danced around the openings to the hoods. The ninth man, the fool playing the violin, was dressed as a priest. For a moment his garb shocked me, though I wasn't sure why. I am not in the least bit religious. I could see the mitre on the back of his head dipping in time to the eerie cadence of his music. The dancers weaved in and out of one another as if they were threading a mystic figure in the dim light of the lamps which the watchers were supposed to recognize. The early jollity had gone from the audience and had been replaced by solemnity.

One of the eight held an open black umbrella over the fiddler, hiding his face in shadow. It was not raining — on the contrary the night was sultry — and the scene should have been humorous. Instead, it struck me as sinister, though I did not understand why.

The music though weird was compelling and I opened the window almost without thinking, to hear it more clearly. It filled my room with its dismal sound and I experienced a familiar feeling. Or was it the same? I looked down instinctively to see if I had picked up the astrolabe unknowingly.

My hand was empty. Yet the feeling persisted. Not the same, but similar. Quickly I shut the window, my sensitivity protected by the leaded glass.

They *were* here then! I sat down on the bed, my hands trembling in my lap. There was a choice to make. I could stay in Thaxted until they contacted me, or I could get in my car and drive. What was I afraid of? I had come on my own accord. They didn't even know I was here.

Or did they? My glance fell on the astrolabe that glinted from the table like a cyclops' eye, watching my deliberations. How had I heard about it? The typewritten postcard that had a Thaxted postmark I had assumed came from the antique dealer. And my dealings with the buyer had been through postal communications. I picked up the heavy disks of metal, smooth as silk with use. Was it one of theirs? Constellations etched upon its plates murmured through my sensitive fingers. Secrets. Secrets.

The telephone buzzed, making me start. I let it ring twice before putting down the astrolabe and lifting the receiver.

"Yes?"

The voice was low and guttural. "The church." Then the line buzzed. Whoever it was had hung up. The music was still filling the room from the outside, faintly persistent. I looked out again and counted the dancers. Seven besides the fool. One was missing.

I waited for about twenty minutes, until the music stopped. Then I began to dress.

Perhaps I was overreacting but I didn't stop to think too hard. I followed my instincts, a natural bent with me. After all, I had no one I need answer to. As I passed Denys' room, she was entering it, presumably having been to the bathroom at the end of the hall.

"Where are you going?" she asked in a surprised tone of voice.

"I just . . . I wanted to take a walk."

She looked down at my hands. I was clutching my shoes.

"Are you mad?" she hissed. "It's gone midnight."

For once I thought she was right about me. I was mad but I was also curiously frightened.

"Look Denys, I don't know why but I'm worried about . . . well something just happened to me which I can't explain. Please, *indulge* me if you think I'm crazy."

Her eyes softened.

"Will you explain later?"

"If I can," I said. I pulled on my shoes. "Look. I'll be back soon. Wait in my room for me. I just want to look around."

She nodded, though she still looked concerned. I couldn't blame her. Something had entered my life which I knew was highly portentous, but I could not explain why, even to myself. I just knew that Thaxted held something for me and I had felt its influence swamping my senses.

I left by the back of the hotel and made my way along the

narrow street towards the church. It meant I had to navigate the midnight-filled alleys. I had no choice however.

With my heart pounding in my chest I walked quickly through the blackness of the Thaxted hinterland. The music was still in my head and with it that unwelcome feeling of being influenced against my desires. Why was I so suspicious? I wasn't entirely sure except that there had been a threat of menace in the music which I was unable to identify — at least, not clearly. Perhaps because I was part of it: an undeveloped version of those dancers?

I had started to cross the main street when the thing came hurtling out of the night to clamp itself on my thigh. It clung there, gibbering, and I screamed out in terror. I tried to swipe the demon to the ground but only glanced it, and its claws dug deeper into my leg. Although I had no wish to see it, I staggered blindly under a street light, almost swooning with the fear that had engulfed me.

It was a monkey — the photographer's animal — its small body shivered nervously against my own, teeth chattering some message of its own fear which was lost on my human ears. Its left arm was entangled with a pair of straps: one attached to a money satchel, the other to the photographer's Polaroid camera. The camera itself was battered and broken, having been dragged along cobbled streets.

As I tried, still shaking, to peel away the poor creature's limbs, it dropped suddenly to the ground. The camera broke into two or three pieces and lay at my feet. The animal itself scuttled off into the darkness, leaving behind the purse.

Slowly I bent down and picked up the pieces of the Polaroid. Where was the photographer? Had his monkey escaped? It had not been chained or roped in any case. Perhaps something had frightened it and it had run away from its master? Perhaps it, too, had felt the menace of that music — a creature more sensitive than a civilized human.

The camera was ruined. I poked a finger into the remains and found a damp piece of card. A photograph? I pulled the picture from its slot. The surface was shining with fluid. It had obviously not long been taken, and the owner had not had time to remove it before . . . before what? Before the monkey had made a mad, unpredictable dash into the night?

I studied the photograph.

The flash had illuminated two of the faces beneath the hoods, and though it would be wrong to say that I recognized them, they did register immediately. Both had that silvery sheen below the eyes and nostrils. I connected them at once with the painting in the guildhall. There was no doubt in my mind whatsoever that they were the same people. *But the painting was several hundred years old!*

I stared at the two faces, seeing them complete for the first time. The expressions were . . . intransigent. There was really no other word which would have fitted. Then I realized there was a third, in the background, between the other two, which had not been previously apparent to me in the poor light. It was like no other face I had ever seen before, and inside I felt as cold as death. How can I describe it? Warped? Twisted? It was as if one was viewing the features through imperfect bottle-glass. They were elongated and spiraled into a barely recognizable caricature of a human face. And inherent in that visage was an ancient and long-wielded *power*.

Here was the lord of the dance: the fool in priest's clothing.

I let the photograph fall to the street and walked quickly to where the car was parked against the church wall. Turning in my head were the lines of Denys' poem:

> *The blast again, ho, ho, the blast!*
> *I go to a mansion that shall outlast;*

I knew now what those lines meant, though I had misinterpreted them before. Like all good poems, "The Wizard's Funeral" was oracular. I had previously taken the simple, most obvious meaning: that the wizard was going to an afterlife. Now the import of the words struck a more chilling chord: the *mansion* was not heaven or hell, or any spiritual house. It was the wizard's rejuvenated body. Not life after death, but life after life.

And the *blast* was not a hot wind coming from another world, it was the sudden excretion of age, like a wave of air rushing outwards, to be absorbed by unsuspecting onlookers.

> *And the stoled priest who steps before*
> *Shall turn and welcome me at the door.*

The fool of the dance. But they needed a medium to permit the flow of age.

The medium was music — an ancient music, older than Christianity, older perhaps than Man. I had felt the blast in my room, standing at the open window. The *danse macabre* was not a dance of death but an annual dance of rebirth. A ritual necessary for the perpetration of a species of a race beyond my present understanding, but a race of which I was, or could be, a member.

Was that what I was? Was that what I wanted to be? Each spring to return to dance at Thaxted amongst tourists and villagers, who would absorb a year of my age into their unsuspecting bones? The skeleton ages, the flesh withers, but who among them would perceive a single, additional year? Each year, the ritual dance. Centuries of years passed on to changing audiences. Most of the villagers would bother to watch the dance only a few times in their lives. Midnight is late for the old to be out. Hardy young men from public house bars and possibly their girlfriends would form the main knot of the watchers. Families with children allowed to remain up after their normal bedtimes — they would be there. And afterwards? I would creep away with my fellow dancers, to live another quiet, stolen year on a farm, or in cottage lodgings, making no ripples in the community that closets me. Moving often from village to village, I would avoid becoming a subject for curious rumour-mongers.

Just living, living, living endless grey days.

I would be able to permit no accidents. My body would be more precious than a star. Nothing more than quiet walks, meetings in inns with my ancient fellow wizards: old eyes staring into old eyes. Did I want a face of bottle-glass? Lines in my brow deeper than knife grooves in the trunk of a thousand-year-old yew? Dust in my hollow bones older than the crumbling gravestones of the dead? There would be murders when humans stumbled too close to truth. Protection of eternal life would become a ruthless occupation, a necessary task of evil sages.

Did I want to exchange Denys for a group of wizened Ancients that coughed foul secrets into my ear? Did I want to replace her companionship with that of ugly contemporaries who thwart the natural onrush of death?

My God, I did not.

My hands were trembling as I fumbled for the car keys. For a terrible moment I thought I had forgotten them. Then I had them in my hand and was soon sitting behind the wheel. As the engine coughed to life, I caught a glimpse of someone on the far side of the churchyard. A figure moving quickly, head down, behind the stone wall. I drove the Lancia out into the street, the wheels shrieking as I overaccelerated in my haste to get to The Argus. Outside the hotel the streets were now empty.

I jumped out quickly and ran around the back where I had left the door unlocked. My skull had a numb feeling as a single thought pressed against its walls: *was Denys still safe?*

She was not in her room. I almost screamed for the second time that night. Then I heard a sound along the corridor and went quickly to my own room. Denys was there, lying on my bed. She looked up at me sharply as I grabbed her wrist.

"We have to leave," I said. "Some people are after me. I can't explain now but we're in danger."

There was an urgency to my voice, but I was calmer now that she was with me. She looked into my face, which must have reflected my fears.

"But ... all right," she said.

I threw her a pair of my slacks and a sweater. When she had them on, we descended the stairs, swiftly, but I felt I had control of myself now. Someone called from one of the other rooms, possibly the landlord's. We ignored it. The motor was still running as we scrambled into the car, and I pulled away smoothly from the curb, without the squeal this time.

"God. ...." began Denys, but I said, "Wait. Not yet," and she shut up immediately.

The town seemed deserted until we reached the outskirts, where a solitary figure stood in the centre of the road. Leaning forward, Denys said, "It's the police."

I pressed my foot instinctively on the brake and prepared to stop.

Then something, a small internal warning, made me flick the headlamp switch. The full beams came on and illuminated the policeman's face. There was a reflection: facial patches of snail tracings I now knew and feared.

I rammed my foot on to the accelerator and we swept past him, brushing him with the side of the car and spinning him off his feet. I didn't even pause to look in the rearview mirror. I felt Denys' eyes on me, and I gave her a sideways look before concentrating on the road ahead.

Soon we reached the main highway. I heard a click and glanced down to see something in Denys' hands.

"The astrolabe," she said. "After all, that's what we went to Thaxted for. You didn't want to leave it behind, did you?"

"No," I replied, shaking my head. I had left something else behind.

I wondered what she would say if I told her I had traded eternity for her companionship.

The car sped on towards London.

LET'S GO TO GOLGOTHA!

The Time-Travel Agency was the third room along one of the branches of a Banyan building. It was a long way up, and it took Simon Falk a considerable time to reach the pink glass doors. A notice outside read, PAN PACKAGE TOURS OFFER YOU THE REMARK-ABLE! THIS IS YOUR CHANCE TO SEE THE BATTLE OF MARATHON, THE WARS OF THE ROSES, THE FIRST MANNED SPACE FLIGHT. ABSOLUTELY NO PERSONAL RISK. Simon stared into the interior and then went, reluctantly, it seemed, inside. An assistant slid silently to his side the moment he was in the room, with hands clasped before him in deference to his customer. Perhaps he was requesting aid from above, thought Simon, to get him through his potential sale?

"Can I help you, sir?"

Simon knotted his own fingers behind his back to even the balance and to hint gently that he was not yet ready to buy.

"Just some brochures, please. Can I take some away with me to, er, study at leisure?"

"Certainly, sir." The fingers unravelled themselves and began deftly plucking multi-coloured sheets of paper from the display shelves with the expertise of a seasoned fruit-picker.

"When you and your . . . ?"

"Family," Simon finished for him.

"Precisely!" The words were neat and well cared-for. Trimmed to the correct length and each separated by a time pause fitting for the intended effect. "When you have made your minds up," he continued, "perhaps you will give us a call and we will see what can be arranged. There is no need to come personally for the booking . . ."

Simon wriggled uncomfortably. "I was just on my way home — I know I could have ordered them by mail but my wife is impatient."

"Yes," the salesman smiled silkily. "Um, the Coronation of Elizabeth the First is fully booked, I'm afraid, and the Revolution of Mars has only a limited number of seats available."

"I don't believe we are too interested in those events," said Simon.

"Your first time, sir?"

"Yes, as a matter of fact it is."

"Then may I recommend the Sacking of Carthage? We mingle with the camp followers on a neighbouring slope. However, I must add that it's not for the squeamish."

Simon asked, "Isn't that a little dangerous?"

"Er, no, not as long as you follow our little instructions." The agent wagged a finger playfully. "We've never lost a customer yet."

Simon murmured his thanks and almost ran out of the room. He hated these pre-holiday forays, but he owed his family a vacation and they were going to get it. It had to be one of these time-tours: he could not afford space travel. There was nothing else to do. Earth was a solid block of brick and concrete flourishing with Banyan buildings, and ocean cruises made his children ill. He stepped out of the building and hailed a floater, avoiding the blast of the air purifiers as he crossed the tiled roof to meet it.

Mandy was waiting at the door of their flat in the same mantis-like attitude employed by travel agents.

"Did you get the brochures?"

He sighed a resigned sigh. "Yes, I got them."

She grabbed at the wad. "Wonderful, let me see them. Oh, don't look so depressed, you know you always enjoy it once we get away. A trip through time!" She clutched the brochures to her breast. "I'm going to love every minute of it."

"Well, I hope it'll be up to your expectations," Simon said dryly. "It's going to cost us enough, and my business is not doing as well as it should." He trailed his sentence over to the cocktail cabinet, and made himself a drink.

"Oh, tish," she replied. "A holiday will do you good. You'll come back full of fresh ideas and thoroughly relaxed." She turned over some of the brochures in her hands. "We don't want anything too violent — it might upset the children."

Simon gave a snort. "The children would wallow in it. James likes nothing better than the sight of blood, and Julie would rather see a space war picture than a live ballet performance."

"Don't be cynical, dear. Anyway, that's all the more reason to get them away," protested Mandy. "They have nothing else to do but play on the rooftops these days."

"Nothing else to do," he cried, overdoing the incredulous tone. "Did I have underground free-play fairgrounds when I was a boy? Did you have . . . ?"

"Oh, don't start that again. When will you understand that children cannot appreciate what they have always had? Let them see how children lived in other ages, other countries." Mandy paused. Then she continued, "We should have shown them before. Perhaps we should take them to Sparta. Did you know that the children of Sparta were placed in military academies at the age of eight and told to steal their food or starve? The crime was getting caught. I wonder what our children would think of the boy that let a fox gnaw on his abdomen rather than let his elders discover he had stolen it, and had hidden it up his smock?" Her blue eyes searched his face for signs of agreement.

"They would probably think he was a damn fool, and so do I," Simon replied.

She tried again. "Perhaps we should take them to Rome . . . ?"

"Or Pompeii the day before it erupted — and leave them there."

"Don't be nasty. What about the Holy Land . . ."

". . . at the time of the Crusades," finished twelve-year-old James, who had entered the kitchen eating.

"Not before your dinner, James," complained his mother. "Your father and I will decide where we are going — go and wash your hands. Where's Julie?"

"She's coming."

That evening Simon and Mandy Falk sat at the table poring over brochures and fighting over places, prices and dates until the front door sang softly, telling them that their closest friends were waiting to enter the house. Simon pressed a switch and shortly afterwards Harry and Sarah Tolbutt entered the room.

"Hello, hello, holiday time again?" chirped Harry, unzipping his outerwear suit.

Simon smiled and scratched the bridge of his nose.

"Yep. We can't decide where to go. Or should I say *when* to go? It's a bit confusing."

"If you are talking about time-tours, why don't you come with us? We're going to see the Crucifixion," said Sarah, with a little flick of her head.

"The what!" cried the Falks together.

"The Crucifixion of Christ," said Harry nonchalantly. He became earnest. "You see, we thought the children needed to see exactly what happened so that they had a real understanding of religion and what it means. You know what children are like."

"We know," said Simon in a hollow tone.

Sarah continued. "If they could see exactly how Jesus died to save us — or our souls or whatever it was that he saved — it might have a profound effect on them. At least, we hope it will."

Simon began mixing the drinks.

"Isn't it a bit sacrilegious?" he said quietly. "I mean, after all . . ."

Harry spoke again. "Well, I suppose on the surface it does seem a bit ghoulish and bloodthirsty, but as long as one goes with the right attitude I think it is all right. As long as one bears in mind what one is there for."

Mandy said, "Do you know, that is exactly what I was thinking before you came over? Wasn't I, Simon?"

"Yes, I'm a mind-reader," he winked at Harry. Mandy ignored him. "We are drawing too far away from the things that matter in life, like religion."

"You've not mentioned going to church in ten years," scoffed Simon.

Mandy dismissed this remark with a flick of her hand. "That's not important," she retorted. "A pack of old men droning out of the scriptures is not religion. I want to see the real thing — I think we should go, Simon."

Thus it was decided by Mandy and Sarah. Simon, his family and their friends were going to see the Crucifixion, at modest package tour prices, of course.

Pan Time-Tours Limited had its offices in Southend High Square. The Falks and the Tolbutts shared a floater to the pre-tour lecture to economize on the fare. The day was unusually bright for the season and in the floater, protected from the fresh

sea breeze, they were warm and excited. Simon always felt good
on a day when the sun managed to cut its way through the layers
of cloud and he could see it twinkling on the giant floating
platform that launched the starships high above the sky. He had
never been into space. Simon Falk was secretly a confirmed
homebody.

They reached the small lecture hall and took seats inside.
Simon looked around him.

"There's quite a few people here," he whispered to Harry. "Do
you think they are all on our tour?"

"Must be," said Harry. "There's no other lecture booked for
today."

"Can I have your attention, please?" A young, serious-looking
clergyman stood on the small rostrum before them. The
murmuring died down. The vicar was a short man with old-
fashioned glass spectacles. It was an affectation of the clergy. His
glasses flashed like metal discs in the sunlight that fell in stripes
down the east side of the hall.

"First of all, welcome to Pan Time-Tours. I am one of your
Preparation Officers and I am here to give you advice on what to
expect and how you must conduct yourselves." He smiled. "We
do not lay down any rules, but it is important you should know
how to act because on this tour, as on many others, you will be
mixing with the locals. You must be inconspicuous — this is the
primary rule."

One or two hands shot up, but the clergyman waved them
down.

"Now, I know a lot of you will have questions, but I must ask
you to be patient. We will give you time at the termination of the
lecture to get your queries answered. Many of them will probably
be dealt with as the lecture continues. We have done this all
before."

He looked up and smiled again. The sunlight from the window
struck his left cheek, smearing it with holy gold, and the audience
settled comfortably in their soft chairs.

"You will all be issued with the appropriate clothing before you
embark, and everyone will go through our treatment room to
ensure that their outward appearance does not clash with that of
the natives. This is a perfectly harmless process and is easily

reversible on return from your holiday. We can't have any giant
Nordic blondes standing out like poorly disguised Vikings at a
Ramadan feast. A few days before the trip you will all be invited
to visit our language laboratory, where you will be taught
Hebrew by the knowledge-injection principle during one
afternoon. As you probably know, the knowledge will only last
about a month before it disappears completely from your
brains. We can't stuff it in in two or three hours and expect it to
remain there, otherwise we would all be brilliant."

He gave a soft snigger.

"Can't I be a Roman soldier?" a spotty-faced youth shouted
from behind Simon.

The clergyman reproved the caller with a stern finger and
said gravely, "Sir, I did warn you not to ask questions until the
end. You will be given ample opportunity then. However, I will
give you a reply because I was shortly coming to the importance
of being Hebrews. The tour needs to stay together. A Roman
soldier or two tagging along behind civilians will not look right,
and besides, occupation troops have commitments — they
might be recalled to barracks at short notice. You might be
stopped for dirty buttons or something — a soldier is too
vulnerable. Apart from all this, soldiers act in a particular
fashion and have gestures and phrases peculiar to their
profession — we would be sure to give ourselves away. Take it
from me that we need to go as civilians."

"I don't want to be a Jew," muttered James. Simon nudged
him to be quiet.

The speaker continued. "Now, this last part is most important
— and I shall understand if any of you wish to drop out. If you
do — only at this juncture, mind you — your deposit money will
be refunded. If any of you are thrown in prison for any reason,
we might not be able to get you out in time — that is, before you
disappear into the bowels of a slave galley or end up at the
bottom of the stoning pit."

There was a loud shuffling of feet and muttering of voices
from his audience, and he waited with bowed head until it had
ceased.

"There is no risk," he continued, "providing you do exactly as
you are told. I cannot stress the importance of this too much.

You know what happened and how it happened. We will arrive on the day that Pilate asks the inhabitants of Jerusalem whom he should set free, as the citizens are permitted to grant amnesty to one prisoner over the Feast of the Passover. When the crowd begins to shout 'Barabbas', as we know it must, then you must shout it too. You must not appear to be different in any way from the rest of the citizens. This is vitally important. You have to appear to be in agreement with the rest of the crowd. You must jeer at Christ and shake your fists as he drags the cross through the streets. You must remember that communities in those times were not very large, and if a small section of people is silent the others will begin to wonder why and will question you. You will be sure to give yourselves away under stress — not because you are idiots but because you are clever. People in those times were simple. They followed the ring-leaders, and they will regard anyone who does not with great suspicion. It is far more difficult to think and speak with simplicity under pressure than it is the reverse, so do as I say and everyone will be perfectly safe. It may be distasteful and even repugnant to your nature, but it is a necessity. When they nail up the sign 'Jesus of Nazareth, King of the Jews', you must laugh. Those that remain awestruck while the rest of the crowd are dancing and prancing, screaming and shouting, will only draw attention to themselves by their silence. I repeat, it is for your own safety. Now, are there any questions?"

The sermon was at an end. Only two childless couples asked for a refund of their deposit.

"How could they do that?" asked Julie for about the fifth time, just before they left for Jerusalem. "How could they crucify him? His own people. The same people that cheered and threw palm leaves before his feet such a short time before. It's like giving someone a ticker-tape parade and then hanging him."

"I don't suppose that is unknown either," replied Simon.

The children, after their initial reluctance to enjoy the pre-holiday plans, had settled down to the idea and had been studying their Bibles.

"Don't forget what the man said, they were a very simple people."

Simon was pleased with Julie. She was going with the right

objectives in mind: to study the people who had executed Christ and to attempt to analyse their motives.

Julie went on, "I can't believe they *had* to do it. I know Christ had to die to save us all from sin but ..."

"It was mankind that was to blame. You must think in general terms. You can't blame individual nations like the Romans or the Jews."

"Well, I still think it is terrible, the way they treated him."

Yes, Simon was well pleased with Julie. He was not too sure about James yet. James was a deeper one than Julie and had to be plumbed over a longer period of time than had been available.

The treatment room, as promised, was painless, and the journey itself was almost a delight. It left you with a slightly dizzy feeling but if you kept your eyes closed the sensation was that of sliding down a seemingly endless helter-skelter. There really was nothing to it. When Simon opened his eyes he found himself sitting on warm sand beside a narrow goat track. The others were in the positions they had held inside the time room. They all climbed to their feet and made their way along the goat track towards the town that shimmered in the heat in the distance. The sun pressed hot on the backs of their necks and Simon put an arm round James to stop him from stumbling. None of them were used to walking on uneven ground covered in sharp stones. Simon felt sorry for some of the older members of the party.

The courier entered the town first. He was recognizable by his matted hair, rags and the ancient staff he carried, but no one was to speak to him except in dire emergency. The walk was a long one and the rough smocks were uncomfortable. Several children were beginning to complain of the heat and that their skins were sore where the cloth was rubbing, but there was a general atmosphere of excitement pervading the adults. At least we look authentic enough, thought Simon. The smocks and sandals were genuine, bought on a previous trip by a Tour Preparation Officer. Some of the members had elected to go barefoot at the request of the firm. Their feet had been hardened during the process in the treatment room. Nevertheless, thought Simon, they will be raw by the time we go back. Presumably Pan Time-Tours relied on the suffering of Christ to overawe the visitors and make them

ashamed of their own trivial problems. A dog ran in and out of
their legs, barking, as they trailed down a narrow dusty street.
Their first meeting with one of the locals. Simon glanced at
Mandy. Her new brown eyes flashed at him, and she looked very
beautiful in a gypsyish sort of way.

"Glad you came?" she whispered in Hebrew.

"I don't know yet," he said in all seriousness.

Finally they passed between some hard mud dwellings and out
into a square in the middle of the town.

"Just in time," said the courier. "Spread out, everyone."

The mob was dense, but Harry procured a clear place just
inside the periphery of the crowd. A tall, thin man with an
intelligent face was addressing the people from the steps of a
stone building. He looked harassed and a little ill. He was
speaking in Latin.

"What is he saying?" whispered Simon to Harry, who had
studied the classics in his youth.

"He is asking us to choose the one to go free," answered Harry.
"You know, you've read the book."

"Oh," said Simon.

The crowd shuffled but remained silent. A fly settled on the end
of Simon's perspiring nose and he flicked it away impatiently.
God, it was hot, he thought. The Roman repeated his previous
sentence. Suddenly, as if he had just comprehended the question,
James cried out "Barabbas!" in a high voice. He had been day-
dreaming, and the question, as did many questions in Latin in the
classroom at school, had taken him off his guard. The sound
echoed over the hard, baked square, and James looked a little
frightened at his outburst. Then the mutterings in the crowd
began, and soon everyone was yelling.

"Barabbas! Barabbas!"

Simon felt relieved that the shouting had started. He had been
startled by his son's yell and was afraid that attention had been
drawn to them. No one was looking at them, however.

"What did you do that for?" he hissed under the uproar.

James was nervous and tense.

"I'm sorry. I thought we were supposed to. He asked us and the
man said . . . I don't know."

"Never mind," intervened Harry. "It would have happened

anyway. You just jumped the gun, that's all. Don't do it again, though, or we may be in trouble."

James looked miserable, but Simon let it go at that. There was no sense in causing a scene, and what was done was done. They stood for about an hour in the square, with none of them quite sure what was happening, and then Julie said she felt sick. Simon and Mandy took her behind one of the strawbrick houses, leaving James with Harry and Sarah and their children.

"It must be the heat," said Mandy after a while. "It's getting at me a bit too. Couldn't we sit down somewhere in the shade?"

She looked down the narrow street for somewhere to rest but there was nothing in view. Then, having an idea, she walked over to one of the houses and looked in from the open doorway. A Hebrew family was sitting on stools in the middle of the room with their hands clasped in front of them. The old man of the group raised his eyes inquiringly. It was cool in the doorway, but it was obvious that she was intruding on something very private.

"Sorry," said Mandy, and stepped back into the street. The heat from the ground came up through the soles of her sandals again and she walked on to the next house. It was also occupied: so was the next, and the next. She returned to where Simon and Julie stood.

"There's something funny here," she whispered to Simon when she reached him. "The houses have people in them."

"So?" said Simon in an irritated tone.

"Well, one would think they would be out on a day like today. Why aren't they watching Christ pull his cross through the streets? All the other inhabitants are."

"Perhaps they are ... Well, I don't know. What's the point?" Then he looked thoughtful. "You know, you have something there. Let's check a few more of the houses."

They went from house to house, through dozens of streets, peering into doorways, looking through curtains until they knew they had covered a large portion of the town. Enough to know that there was something terribly wrong. The realization of what that wrong was began to sink in very rapidly, and no matter how hard Simon's mind tried to reject it or concoct excuses to cover it, the awful thought remained. Julie followed her agitated parents, not understanding and obviously unwell.

"I want a drink," she finally complained.

"Well, you can't have one," snapped Mandy. "The water isn't fit to drink. It's got all sorts of germs in it."

"These people are all right," Julie sniffed to deaf ears.

Simon felt a hot wave of air pass over his face. His eyes were sore, his mouth felt dry, and the dust was mixing with the sweat on his feet to form a slimy grime between his toes. His physical discomfort, however, was nothing compared to his mental stress. He felt very afraid.

"Doesn't it strike you as peculiar that the crowd was so large?" he asked, wiping his brow with his sleeve at the same time.

Mandy's voice was taut. "Well, it has been boosted by time-tours from the future. There's more than one agency, don't forget."

Simon was visibly trembling now. "There are dozens of agencies," he cried. "And all the inhabitants of this town are in their houses, praying. Quickly, we've got to find Harry and the others."

Simon grabbed Julie and swung her on to his back. They ran through the streets with the perspiration dripping from their eyebrows and their eyes stinging with the salt and dust. In the distance they could hear the crowd chanting and jeering; they could hear the shrieks of laughter and high-pitched catcalls. It was an ugly, frightening sound, like the screaming of monkeys as a lion pads beneath their trees. It was the forced laughter of hyenas that circle the lion's den at a safe distance as the lord lies, unconcerned, in the warm sun. Then, suddenly, there was silence.

Simon slowed, gasping for breath. He could see the rut made by the corner of the cross snaking along the street and disappearing into the distance. A shudder went through him.

"My God," he sobbed to his wife, "we've killed him."

A sandal slipped from his foot as he ran but he disregarded it. He felt none of the sharp stones that cut the soles and heels of his feet.

The pair of them stumbled on, following the tell-tale mark in the dust, until they reached the crowd. The faces were all turned in one direction and wore expressions of shocked sympathy.

Simon did not dare look towards the crosses. He knew he would faint if he did, and he had seen the shadows out of the corner of his eye. It was enough. They found Harry and Sarah and the children on the edge of the crowd, as silent and watchful as the others. Sarah's cheeks were blotched with white and Harry's mouth was half-open.

"Harry," choked Simon, as quickly as his emotion would allow, "Harry, we've got to get him down."

Harry's stunned mind took time to register the fact that Simon was with them once more. He did not take his eyes from the man on the centre cross.

Licking his lips, he replied helplessly, "Can't do it, Simon. It's got to happen, you know. This is the way it is, but, my God, I wish we had never come. He looked at me, you know. I'll never forget his eyes as long as I live. They were so . . ." he paused to find a word, ". . . so deep."

Simon was frantic. "Harry, Harry. Look at the crowd! Look around you! There are no Jews here. No natives. The only ones here are us. The holiday-makers. Do you realize the enormity of what we've done? The whole guilt of mankind rests on our shoulders."

He was sobbing violently now. "We've crucified the Son of God, and we're going to do it next tour, and the next and the next . . ."

"For ever and ever, time without end, amen," finished Harry, humbly.

SUMI DREAMS OF A PAPER FROG

bamboo

one of the comforting things about being in a war is, you know it isn't real. especially night sentry. you work, eat and sleep so close to death, you become part of it, and everyone knows that death isn't real. death is another world, the final unknown country of the soul and those sort of places are fantasy. death to me is a place of shadows, a dark river flowing through a dark land. and quiet. unnaturally quiet, unreal.

night sentry never made any sense to me. you stand out in the open, as exposed as a carton on a wall, waiting to be punctured. a kind of sacrifice to a killer with random tastes. if he didn't kill you, it was like being lucky at russian roulette. it couldn't last indefinitely. all you could hope for was a stay of execution. a near miss. or that it would be the man next to you. every night. ostensibly you are guarding stores, or ammunition, or 'planes, but you know the enemy has enough of his own. what he wants is death. mine, yours, anyone's but his and his kind. so we oblige him by standing men outside in the open, inviting his mark. it would have made more sense to protect the men, using the supplies to build a barricade around them, surrounding them while they live out their individual fantasies. then they would only dream of being a naked target on a wide landscape. they wouldn't be silhouettes. cardboard cutouts.

you spend these long, long night hours — a lifetime of hours — wondering what the enemy is like out there. staring into the darkness you wonder if he will appear as a man or like some terrible angel, spitting death through his teeth. the other night i saw a man die. he slapped his face as if he'd been bitten by a mosquito, then he seemed to fold in on himself, like a paper doll pressed by an unseen hand. it seemed i stood there for an age, staring at his body without comprehending. then i put out my hands, palms outwards into the night and said, "no". just that, as if i could protect myself from their weapons with the power of a gesture.

if the chances of being killed on night sentry are high, the odds shorten considerably if you smoke a cigarette. there are a dozen reasons, beyond this survival factor, why you shouldn't smoke. it is forbidden and carries heavy penalties: extra night duties.

if you are holding a cigarette in your hand, it increases the time it takes to aim your rifle. the smell of smoke carries miles and however hard you try to blanket the lighted end with your hand the small red dot will be visible to the enemy at some time. other reasons. yet you still smoke. you smoke because you are afraid of the possibility of dying and you turn that possibility into a probability by smoking. you also smoke because you are bored. you are bored *and* afraid, and these two emotions are entirely compatible. they interlace in the unreal wickerwork of war.

i always think of the enemy as bamboo. there are 1000 varieties of bamboo in the world and that might be the number of guises the enemy adopts. bamboo is strong and resilient. it grows thick, fast and replaces itself rapidly. it is segmented and it has a thousand uses, from prison bars to chess pieces to kendo swords. it is the peasant and the king. it is hollow, it is a native of this land. it is invincible.

i always think of the enemy as bamboo.

paper

i always think of myself as paper. a product of slim fingers skilled in origami. so, i have the appearance of a real creature but i am really only folded paper filled with air, wounds cannot harm me, are not fatal, nothing but total destruction will affect my life force. if i can believe this i am safe.

on night sentry, the rifle weighs heavy in your arms. there are many left-handed sentries. this is because the bolt, with which you cock the weapon, protrudes from the right side of the rifle: thus it can be hooked on the belt and bear the weight. the rifle weighs eleven pounds. over a period of two hours the poundage increases alarmingly but always the weapon must be pointed out into the night. this is in the regulations.

the enemy must be given all the advantages. a noise, a shape, an approach, must all be challenged three times before you are permitted to defend yourself. this is in the regulations.

for me, all sounds are the enemy. inhibited by a conventional upbringing however, i never issue a challenge. i merely stand, listening for further sounds to confirm my fears. when *those* sounds come i wait for more. sometimes i listen so hard it hurts my ears. once, a comrade called out

"halt, who goes there?"

and i almost shot him for filling my head with sound while i was listening for the enemy. instead, *they* shot him, a second later. i was on a hill and he was below. he fell across the barbed wire fence and hung there, like biltong drying in the moonlight, until we could bring him up at first light.

you learn to beware of beauty. many sunsets pass before your eyes, and many dawns, mostly beautiful but all treacherous. with dusk and dawn comes twilight. half-light is worse than no light. it tricks the eyes with its strange movements. also a false sense of peace security. you relax, allow the redness of the sky to engulf you, and it will engulf you. it does to remember the colour of blood.

foolishness does not start and end with twilight. i have seen beauty at night, formed out of arcing lights. silent, white pieces of brilliance have made rainbow curves over my head and i have wonderingly admired them. when there is no accompanying sound it takes more than a few seconds to recognize tracer, even when it is aimed at you. afterwards your teeth chatter with the cold and your shirt soaks up the sweat. beauty betrays you to death. i am wary of all colours but black.

glass

you may use the night glasses to search for the enemy along distant treetops. he is always nearer than the point you watch. i never use the night glasses. they have within them an even stranger world of fantasy than the one of which i am already part. they show you a grey sham world within the black night, where resemblances live. a tree is a man holding out his arms. a rock is a man hunched against the ground. the figures move within the glass. they move because the hand that holds them moves. or they move because they really are men.

no one has ever seen a real man through night glasses. real men don't exist inside them, or they do, and the watcher, the man with the glass in his hand, he doesn't exist. it doesn't matter which way it is. the result is oblivion.

drum

the loudest part of my body is my heart. it fills the night with its pounding. they can hear the beating in a far off country called "home". there are other, smaller drums all over my body. in my wrists, my ears, wherever you walk the drums go with you, signalling your position to the enemy. your body has other giveaway noises. sometimes you hear the "crack" of a dry stick snapping and start like a dog at a gunshot. then realize it is one of your joints, an elbow or knee. at other times you can hear your eyelids batting together, as a moth at a lamp. once, an explosion stopped all the drums of my body in midbeat. i broke wind. at such times it is difficult to remember you are paper and nothing can hurt you.

ink

the blackest nights are the brightest.

frogs

they eat frogs here. they tie each limb to a stick and dry the creature in the sun, before cooking it over a fire.

fires

you can be forgiven, sometimes, for believing in reality, when there are fires like red flowers a long way off in the night, and you can hear the "whumph" of distant mortars, the crackle of gunfire, out over the bay. you can be forgiven for thinking that the world is real. that's because the activity appears to be nothing to do with you. it can't touch you, you are safely cocooned by two miles of night and the fear leaves you.

then it all seems real. this is an illusion which is provoked by unguarded moments. before long the silence will drift in with the moonlight and the fires will go out. then your complacency dissipates and the cold fantasy returns. reality is only a dream. behind the lines, there is much to reinforce your belief in fantasy. the atrocity reports that are broadcast each day, of crucifixions and human torches, cannot be real. they are so grisly, so horrific, the enemy must have one of their kind, a man with a terrible imagination, whose responsibility it is to develop these graphic, fictional executions. perhaps in this war no one is *ever* actually killed. perhaps, overnight, they invent the figures of the dead.

"between the hours of midnight and six o'clock, the front for the liberation of the people shot and killed seven of the enemy."

then, to consolidate the lie, seven men act out their deaths and are taken away from our sight. each supposed death you see confirms this belief. men do not actually die, they merely drop loosely to the earth with the faintest of sighs, their bodies empty of breath. why don't they scream, clinging to life with fingers like claws? the grapevine adds further confirmation. you hear that joe is dead, decapitated by cheesewire between rockets fired in tandem. then, behind the lines three weeks later you see joe on the beach, sunning the face he is said to have lost. none of this is real. this makes it easier for you to be paper.

there are women behind the lines. nurses and welfare ladies. through the glasses you watch them undress at night. your stomach kicks and your throat feels as if a three-inch nail is caught in the windpipe. their breasts have the appearance of alabaster wrapped in tissue. then they unwrap them and unwittingly display them for your benefit. there are a hundred exhalations into the night. the shadows hide multiples of you. but, these are not real women. they are ethereal figures trapped between the lenses of the glasses. occasionally you puzzle over the casing of the binoculars, wondering how they managed to manufacture such wonderful interpreters of need. yet, it is an agony of pleasure. a single glimpse may take two or three hours of waiting. this is not sex, it is nostalgia. nostalgia makes your heart perspire, not your hands, and in your breast the static builds, to be released in a shower of fine, internal sparks when the vision has gone.

death

there is a fantasy deeper than death: the fantasy of capture and subsequent torture. i didn't hear them, which still puzzles me because i was attentive, wary. suddenly, he was beside me and i looked into his face and almost greeted him, as one would a stranger who had stopped to ask directions. his face was round, without a smile but not savage with malice: just round, and pleasant. then the whip of bamboo on the back of my neck.

i awoke stretched between the four poles. a frog. a paper frog. i stare at the sky and my belly arches up to meet it. this is because of the bamboo rods which puncture my paper back.

home, too, is now a fantasy. its grasp on reality has slipped and now it is with me in my make-believe world. since it is not real now, it never was. my memories of that place that never was are inventions of my mind. there was never a face with blue eyes and blonde hair. there never were two children laughing, except in my head. my mind is full of old photographs of non-existent features.

around me i hear domesticity: the scraping of spoons in tins. i can smell cooked fish. inside me is a continuous internal pain which is so unvarying that it slips beyond my awareness, like the eternal high note of a song, so that i have to concentrate to bring it back to me. i have borrowed this pain. sometimes i stare at a point in the sky and think, "that must be where the pain belongs" because i know it doesn't belong to me. the pain cannot be mine because i am paper, folded into the form of an amphibious creature. someone has puffed air into my rectum to give me this bulbous shape. inside i am nothing but stale breath: a hollowness punctured by the sharp tips of two dozen bamboo rods. the bamboo is still growing and spiky leaves brush my folded-edge limbs. the live rods bear me up, like an offering, to riverwet cloud hippos.

bamboo will grow an inch an hour. flutes, bows and duelling staves. tough as tortoiseshells. sharp as fine, stiff hair. baskets, blowpipes, and scarecrows. strong as malachite. smooth as serpents. candles, boats and cradles. they cut deep slits in my back and pushed the tips inside. i am borne high. the enemy thinks he has a man but all he has is a paper frog. i allow him to believe in his fantasy as i swell, slowly, to draw him inside me.

i will engulf him.

SCARLET FEVER

Mendel was unhappy. His pale, waxen hands formed tulip shapes as he emphasized a point. Occasionally the fingers opened like petals, quickened in action by rapidly passing days and nights. They were poet's hands, fascinating slender tools manipulated directly by his soul. No anatomic connections — muscles, nerves, brain cells, blood, sinews — could be responsible for such beautiful movements. The fingers were controlled straight from the heart: his spiritual heart. His hands held my attention, told me more of the truth than the passionate voice behind their liquidity.

"You see," he said, as we sat side by side watching the shutters go down over the panels in the city's pyramidal roof, "There's so much contentment about — it's impossible to produce vibrant, imaginative poetry. We're all so well looked after . . . no weather to concern us, no fatal illnesses, no overcrowding, no famine — everything completely under control. How can I write, without experiencing something other than *comfort*? You, being a woman, must see how impossible it is."

I, being a woman (which had nothing whatsoever to do with seeing anything beyond what was fact, but Mendel insisted that women were sensitive, intuitive creatures by nature), did not understand his reasoning. If comfort was a problem it would have to be eliminated. I saw no barriers to his art in our cosseted state. If one had to create imagery — well then, these were images. We went unclothed within a cocoon of plasticity: our world was a pyramid's interior, the base of which was forty thousand square miles of symmetry.

Around us moved the inhabitants of a vast waterworld that covered two-thirds the height of our pyramid. Only the apex surmounted the surface.

Harsh sunlight was filtered. Cold nights excluded. Death was merely an unpleasant, painless duty to be encountered beyond 120 years of age.

"Why don't you write about death?" I suggested, hoping to please him.

"Death, death," he groaned. "Who *hasn't* written about death? Love and death have been written about more times than they've been experienced. For every man that dies or falls in love ten poems have been penned on the same subject. I want *originality*."

"Shall we stroke?" I asked, placing my hand in his lap upon the poet's narrow maleness, still tall as a shaven spike after our recent lovemaking. "Sometimes it helps you."

Shaking his head but making no move to remove my hand, he said sadly, "No."

After a short while he said, "You are very rhythmic, Lethelia. Perhaps that's why we love so well together. I think perhaps I might write a poem on rhythm." It pleased me, as it was intended. The reciprocation was as pleasant as his words.

Afterwards he said, "I have something to show you. Contraband goods. In my apartment."

I felt the pace of my heart quicken. What was he saying? That there was something illegal in his rooms? What would be illegal? He was excited, I could tell by those hands that had so recently stroked such fever into my cleft thighs: they were clenched now, in strength.

"Show me," I said, rising with him, and taking his right hand I placed it possessively under my arm, close to my breast.

He said, "You must keep my secret. The poetry will still be my own — albeit the product of a heightened mind. Others might not understand."

That was it then. Common drugs. I felt disappointed. Not only in him because he seemed about to make compromises but in the realization that nothing was new. But then I remembered. Contraband. Illegality. Something had to be different. Above us the final panels had been shuttered. The artificial light, soft and warm, had increased its luminosity so subtly I had not noticed its presence. We passed others in the street, some in pairs, some alone. Not one of the men had hands to match my poet's and I outfaced the frank appraising stare of any women with confidence. I was rhythmic — Mendel had told me so. In me were the rhythms of the earth and oceans. Let them eat out their hearts.

In the apartment Mendel showed me his secret: an empty vial. Being a poet he surrounded himself with antiques and in his room, dimly lit for the purpose of creating atmosphere, I asked him if the ancient bottle was an acquisition for his collection.

"No," he replied. "The bottle isn't old. Its contents were. *I have drained it with my lips.*"

The sentence was delivered too dramatically to be in the way of ordinary words. Why did he say *drained*, not *drank*? How else would he drink but with his lips? He was waiting, I could see, for me to question him, his lean, white face thrust forward, near to my own.

"What did it contain? What was it that you drank?"

"A liquid containing live bacteria," he said, triumphantly.

I stared into those bright eyes. Was he mad, my poet?

Timidly, I asked, "What kind of bacteria?" wondering if he would fly into a rage, saying, "What difference does it make?" or, "Do you have to pry so keenly? Isn't it enough that I give you most of myself?"

Instead he replied, "A good question, for it makes all the difference. It was a streptococcus — the same that caused the disease *scarlatina* when it was rife. I need a fever, Lethelia. My body lacks passion and my mind is slow. I want it to race with wild, uncontrollable thoughts. I want demons to visit the house of my brain. I want to hallucinate under the influence of scarlet fever — a Godsent, natural condition that will produce a fervour, a tumult of hot dreams."

"Where did you obtain this . . . this fever bacteria?" I had never heard of scarlatina, though of course I knew of the more famous fevers, such as malaria. History books did not protect our innocent minds from such horrors.

"I stole it — from a laboratory. There were many coloured bottles, many beautiful diseases, but I chose this one for its high feverish content. Poetry, poetry — ah, what *ideas* will flow from my pen after this. Look!" He invited me to inspect his neck. In the dim light of the lamps I could see nothing. I told him so.

"You will, you will," he said. "Soon the fever will come, and then tiny red spots each surrounded by an areola of pink, starting at the neck. They will cover my whole body." He became matter-of-fact. "I want you to nurse me — through my illness. No doctors, you understand. Just you and I. I want you to promise that. You may wear protective clothing," he conceded. "I don't expect you to be infected. You have no need of inspiration."

"Will this give you inspiration?" I asked wonderingly, foolishly.

The rage came to his eyes but the excitement of the moment overcame it.

"Of *course* it will. No more banality. Visions. Phantoms. Fantastical happenings woven out of the subconscious. It will still be *me* but the inner me. Back there ..." he tapped his cerebellum, ". . . are live, hidden beasts — poems to be interpreted by these hands. The fever will release them. St John was visited by a *religious* fever — I must employ an illness to produce my revelations."

Saint John was the name of our city. He had foreseen the coming of the flood which had covered the Earth. Some said that our city was watertight by accident, not design, but others questioned whether accidents were not in themselves inspired by God.

"Read me the verses," I begged. "I love to hear you recite. Your voice is so *passionate*."

Mendel smiled, reaching for a Bible from the shelf with his tapering fingers. It was an ancient edition of course. Older than the city. Older than the waters.

Mendel read: "Revelations 8, verses 10 and 11. *'And the third angel sounded, and there fell a great star from heaven, burning as it were a lamp, and it fell upon the third part of the rivers, and upon the fountains of waters; and the name of the star is called WORMWOOD: and the third part of the waters became wormwood; and many died of the waters, because they were made bitter.'* "

"Does it say anything about the flood?" I asked.

"No, but displaced water has to go somewhere. Wormwood fell into the ocean and the waters came in walls across the lands. We are in a valley — here they stayed."

"It's such a beautiful story," I said. "There is such *power* behind the thoughts. A giant star burning out its life in the oceans of the Earth after hurtling down from the reaches of space. Such powerful images."

"Not only beautiful, but true. Your great-grandparents saw the waters, were engulfed by them. And mine. Oh, I know they had long since been ostracized by nature. Even *their* great-grandparents had not touched the outside."

I said, "Will you write such stories? True stories, that lie waiting to be torn from the deepest recesses of your mind? Will you?"

"I shall," replied Mendel, caressing my breasts with gentle strokes. "I shall."

Two days later Mendel had contracted a sore throat. By that time I had obtained a sterilized suit. He was ecstatic, soon to be delirious.

Mendel did not want me to catch scarlet fever, not because he was concerned for my health but because he wished to be unique. He felt that scarlet fever would be wasted on me. Of course, he was right. I was a mathematician and as such I needed a clear head for my work. I needed no fevers. Later he was to change his mind about withholding the disease from me and others like me.

The sore throat was followed by vomiting and finally the fever arrived. It was a wonderful time. Mendel had a temperature of 102 degrees fahrenheit. He sweated beneath heavy sheets, his eyes growing wilder by the minute. He called out in hoarse tones for metal sheets and stylus. And he wrote feverishly. Sometimes the illness took complete control and he thrashed and groaned in his delirium. We burned a censer to heighten the effect.

On the second day, the rash appeared and his body temperature rose still further, to 104 degrees. Writings lay strewn about the apartment. Devils entered and stamped upon the words. I could not see them but Mendel told me they were there. Once, after falling asleep, he woke screaming and shaking with fright. When I asked him what was the matter, he said he had opened his eyes to see a great fist on his pillow that uncurled into a claw-like hand. The thing was covered in coarse hair, had long, filthy nails and on the palm was the tattoo of a hideous face. Mendel said he had not dared to look up along the arm, towards the owner, for fear his heart would seize.

Mendel's tongue was furred throughout the illness — the strawberry-tongue effect, he told me. He appeared to have great difficulty in eating and drinking. His hands, those wonderful tools of creativity and lovemaking, shook and took on a yellowish hue. We made love once, but it was not altogether successful.

Stroking through clothes was less than satisfying. Most of the time he shivered or lay limp and damp in his sheets, allowing me to stroke him but showing little interest. His eyes burned hot in his brow but it was not because of his enjoyment of sex. He was completely infatuated by his illness. Of course he was sick, but he threw himself into his malady with the energetic abandonment one normally reserved for an enthusiastic love affair. It *was* a love affair. Scarlet fever had become his bedmate, was producing unique experiences for him. He was as possessive over his pyrexia as Othello with Desdemona.

On the third day, Mendel complained of a terrible headache and I was asked to sit quietly crosslegged on the floor by his bedside, occasionally to read him his own writings. One wilting hand rested on my covered shoulders, the wrist actually touching, the spotted palm and fingers hanging with tips a fraction from my breast. Mendel stared at the ceiling through the artificial dusk created by his shaded floor lamps. There were always shadows up there, distorted and vague, as if formed out of the incense which poured from its vessel.

I read slowly, in a low voice, putting the emphasis where I felt it should go. The poetry was strange and rambling — but at the same time had clarity and tautness. The words caught in my throat, like small birds, struggling.

". . . the eagle, blind, explodes in white rain."

By the time the last line had been voiced, Mendel was again soaked in his own sweat. His whole body was shuddering with emotion and fever. When the bout ceased he turned his rash-covered face to mine and said, "You think they're inadequate, the verses?"

The question caught me unawares, but I answered truthfully through my gauze mask, "I think they are beautiful — painfully beautiful."

"But . . ." he said, faltering, "they don't make sense. They're just . . . words."

"Not *just* words. You said they would be dreams and nightmares, thrown out by your subconscious to be translated by your hands. How could you hope to understand that which is disgorged by the recesses of a mind millions of years in the making? Can you imagine the thought processes of primal man?

Yet he is there, inside you, along with a million others. They are you, and you they. Such an intricate mechanism, the human hand. It is the stopper to bottled, ancient thoughts. Yet you have managed to uncork some of those cyphers and lay them on a metal page. Is it any wonder they are, at first, incomprehensible. Remember what Whitman wrote? *'... from the clasp of knitted locks ... let me be wafted.'* Death will release all of those cryptographs, but what can you do with them then? The hand is dead too, and cannot write."

His eyes went back to their study of the ceiling.

"Yes, yes, you are right. It is not that the words are senseless, but that our minds are too ignorant to understand their meaning. The brain is a fumbling, inept piece of tissue and barely adequate at such analysis."

Glad that I had managed to avert the destruction of his spirit, I poured us both a cup of absinthe. We drank, mindful of the toast to Professor Wormwood, who had named the star which had struck our Earth. Was it coincidence that the Bible should have been interpreted by fact so accurately? We did not believe so, and thus we drank the oil from the plant wormwood with its bitter taste. We had our world, isolated but free from outside intervention. No one had found our island in the new oceans, if there were those alive to search. Who knew? We had the sun and rain when we wished. The gardens, nestling in the apex, flourished. Upper panels opened and closed, were shuttered or clear. We controlled our environment to a degree our ancestors would have envied. So we toasted the wormwoods — the astronomer, the fiery star, the aromatic shrub. To these three namesakes went our thanks.

"Lethelia," said Mendel, giving me the empty cup. "Please uncover your face."

I did so, trembling slightly.

"Now kiss me."

"Will I not be infected?"

"I wish it. I want you to join me in my happiness."

So I kissed him. Later I took his writings and showed them to other poets in the cellars below the cafés. They discussed them without my opinion, returning a unanimous verdict that they were nonsensical ramblings: the work of an idiot.

"But you know Mendel is not an idiot. He has written poems which have caused critics to place him in the front rank of Saint John's most respected poets."

"Then he has lost his reason," replied one.

"Yes," I cried, "but don't you see? If poets produced only reasoned thoughts, then they would be scientists, philosophers or logicians. He is a *poet*. His hand breathes beauty, not reason."

They studied the poems once more, but still shook their heads in collective incomprehension. Finally, in a panic, I blurted out the secret. I told them of scarlet fever and its part in the production of the poems. They became excited and once more took up the sheets, running their eyes over the words, until at last one cried, "Yes, yes! I see it!" and they were all at once in a fervour of admiration for the work, each trying to outdo the other in the utterance of praise and the exposition of its meaning.

"We must see the poet," they cried and waving the pages of script they trooped to the apartment of my famous lover. There they stole into his sickroom, one by one, and gravely acknowledged Mendel to be the originator of a new and brilliant movement. They were each his disciple, his pupil. They required guidance. One by one, male and female, kissed him solemnly on his lips. Later that night they left, to await the coming of the scarlet fever, the catalyst for the new school of poetry, henceforth to be known as — *Mendel's Movement*.

I stayed with Mendel and continued to nurse him. I forbade any visits after that because though Mendel was still writing, he was visibly growing weaker. The hands were slow and laboured in their task. I did not want him disturbed. His disciples could carry out his work.

Soon afterwards I went through a bout of scarlatina, but my own illness was very much milder than that of Mendel's. I recovered in textbook time, hardly having to take to my bed at all. Mendel continued to grow worse and, despite his protests, I finally called in a doctor. By this time Mendel's urine was scanty and often contained blood. His feet and face were swollen, giving him a gargoylish look. Also he complained of earache.

The doctor's diagnosis was that Mendel's kidneys were seriously inflamed. He would need hospital treatment at once. Mendel refused to be moved and rejected all treatment. Under the law he was perfectly entitled to do so.

I pleaded with him, crying tears into the pillow beside his head, but he was adamant.

"Don't you see," he said, "I *have* to die. I am a romantic. I am young and my hands beautiful. If I allow these fingers to grow old and wrinkled slowly, perhaps arthritic, they will forget me. My poems will be in some dusty library, unread except by curious archivists. This way ... this way I will be a shuttered sunset in their eyes. The panels will close with a snap and I will never grow old. My poetry will have *deeper* meaning because I died for it. Byron, Keats, Brooke, Owen, I will join them in their immortality."

"But surely," I said tearfully, "if your poetry is good enough, you don't need to die for it."

He shook his head sadly, putting his knuckles lightly to my chest. "But Lethalia, poetry is not mathematics. It isn't viewed objectively, but *subjectively*. My death will make *all* the difference. You told me what changes took place in the other poets and critics once you mentioned the scarlet fever. Before that they were uninterested. Oh, I know the poems are good — but they need support to become acceptable. The style is reactionary, the metre and composition too extraordinary. Death will be the foundation which will shoulder my work."

He lay back on his pillow with a look of peace on his face. During his illness he had written 120 poems — the number of years he would have been expected to live if he had not purposely infected himself with scarlet fever. They were subsequently published as the *Scarlet Volume*. Of his pupils, some 13 died of complications brought on by scarlatina, one or two through the fever itself. Amongst the general public, scarlet fever reached plague proportions when irresponsible poets had spread the disease in an orgy of kissing and lovemaking without first warning their partners of the consequences. In later years, it became a mark of distinction to have suffered and survived the illness, though hundreds did die at the time.

Of course, there was misery and sadness but such emotions were enjoyed, quite openly, after having been absent for so many years. It was a time of great enthusiasm and hope. Ideas bubbled from the minds of men and women and creative art reached a pitch unequalled for centuries. Mendel had awakened their souls and his *Scarlet Volume* became a sacred work in many institutions. Mendel's apartment was transformed into a shrine and I became almost a goddess. Many of his poems featured my name and the passions I had been able to arouse in him. I became the personification of his dead hands.

Mendel died in the early hours of the morning. He called out in pain once or twice and as I moved to give him solace, those lovely instruments of his great career reached up towards the shadows on the ceiling, then fell to his sides. The left one fluttered once, then lay still. I knew he was dead. Later that day I had those da Vinci hands severed at the wrists, embalmed and mounted. They now form the centre-piece of his shrine: alabaster, slender creatures that were Mendel, complete.

THE MAN WHO COLLECTED BRIDGES

Visilia is not a planet.

This bold statement at the outset may serve only to irritate cartographers, but it is unquestionably true. The name of the planet is *Gobi* and Visilia is only an ancient city, an enigmatic ruin in which archaeologists like myself play discovery games. (Or rather, in my case at least, non-discovery games.) Visilia had a brief flare of fame which went beyond our solar system when it was first found by the colonists of Gobi. A city built by non-human hands — or whatever — was universal news in those times of fresh spatial conquests. Consequently, for a short time, Visilia was known to most worlds, and Gobi was lost in its glare. Such misinformation was common in those days of far-flung frontiers, and poor communications. It is doubtful whether much of the incorrect material which found its way into reference books and periodicals was ever revised. Part of the problem lay in the vast amount of new data that became available within a relatively short space of time, and the impossibility of accurate documentation and dissemination.

Scaplan, however, took no notice of my quiet insistence that he call my home planet by its given name. He would call everything he saw "Visilian".

"The Visilian climate can be very unpredictable, I'm told," he said.

I studied the striped effect over the faces of the two moons and wished I was more of a meteorological expert.

"It must mean *something*," said Scaplan, shouldering his haversack. "Maybe it's rain?"

"Wishful thinking," I replied. We were by now well inside the vast desert and the heat was almost unbearable. During the long days we rested while the sun cracked the rocks with its white fingers and we travelled by night. Even so, when it was abroad, it hunted us down to our shallow places, filling our lungs with its own burning breath.

"Anyway," I slapped clouds of grey, choking dust from my pack, "this looks like a wadi we're using as a path. It'll flood within an hour — maybe sooner. It's more than half a kilometre to either bank. We'd have trouble making it."

"A kilometre's not far when it's cool."

"It won't be cool." This wasn't altogether true but I'd abandoned uncertain statements with Scaplan. He was swift to retaliate if I appeared to lack confidence.

"In that case it probably means it's going to be hotter tomorrow." He shifted his pack, presumably to a more comfortable position, and his small fat body quivered with the effort. The top of the pack towered over his damp bald head and there were stains on his shirt where he had sweated beneath the straps. Dark patches beneath his eyes glinted in the moonlight with small pinpricks of perspiration. He was not the ideal companion for such an expedition, but then I hadn't chosen him. It had been the other way around.

We had met at the Oasis of Leords on the edge of the Green Strip. He was advertising his destination on his pack. (EARTH-VISILIA read the patch!)

Scaplan had recognized in me another trekker, a kindred walker, and straightaway sat at my table outside the café. He had launched into conversation immediately, as if, because I was carrying a pack like himself, we were part of a brotherhood and he was entitled to instant friendship. My resistance to overbearing people is not strong and I allowed him to extract my destination. From that moment on I couldn't have prevented us from becoming travelling companions even had I the energy to do so. He would have stuck to me through hostility or tolerance. It was ironic that I had chosen to be a field archaeologist in order to escape people like Scaplan.

It transpired that Scaplan had no real interest in the elusive history of the city, as I had, but he belonged to a Bridge Group. Only later was I to find out what that meant. Two nights out into the desert, for want of something to dispel the boredom, I asked him what his group did.

"We collect bridges," he answered simply, as if it were a common hobby. The tone implied that I should be envious.

"Fascinating," I replied, dryly. "You collect bridges. Why not cathedrals?"

He gave a little laugh.

"Oh, I know what you're thinking. You suppose we take pictures of them, or something like that? Not at all. We walk over them. Once we've crossed the bridge it's ours, so to speak. We cross it off our list. We've walked across seventy thousand bridges — my particular group."

His tone dropped and an awed note entered into his voice.

"That's why I'm here. No group has ever attempted the Visilian half-bridge."

The moons were bright that night and I tried to look into his eyes — those small white stones buried deep in the holes above his cheeks — to gauge the seriousness of his remark. All I could see was reverence.

"My group —" He swallowed, probably to clear the dust. "My group saved a long time to send me here. It's a big responsibility. Have you any idea how much a round trip from Earth costs?"

I shook my head.

"Well, it's a lot of money. More than I could earn in a year. Anyway, we drew lots — five hundred of us — and I was the lucky winner. . . ."

I tried to imagine someone else winning that ticket.

"Do you have any young women in your club?"

"*Group*. Yes, several."

I sighed and rolled my sleeping blanket. Several spiders scuttled from beneath and headed for the protection of the rocks.

Then he laughed.

"Oh, I see what you mean. Well, lucky for me — unlucky for you."

We set off, stumbling over the uneven terrain. Soon the rocks began to freeze and become slippery and I hunched inside my hooded jacket, knowing that within an hour or two my bones would ache with longing for the deadly heat of the day. Every now and again there was a crack like a rifle shot as the frost split another stone in two.

Mercifully we didn't speak very much while we were walking and I was spared Scaplan's descriptions of all his petty holdings.

Not the least of which appeared to be his wife. I now knew that she had a mole on her left ankle, had visited Earth's moon three times with another woman friend, and that her favourite dish was mushrooms. I was at present awaiting further promised details concerning the colours she was using to decorate their house on Earth. He had once during his disclosures given me a worried look when I enquired as to the style of her lovemaking, and had terminated the conversation rather abruptly. I had listed that among my few victories. Unfortunately, my weak character soon overrode my boredom and I atoned for my bad manners by asking him about his favourite subject: bridges. On that particular theme he talked well and held my interest. It was only then that the philosopher emerged from behind the creases in his compressed bulk.

"There is nothing quite as sensuous as the gentle curve of an arch," he said. "Not even the rounding of a woman's buttock." (Score one more for the chauvinist.) "The arch bridge was introduced by the Romans — at least, on Earth it was — when they discovered pressure lines in stone shapes. Viaducts and aqueducts — I've crossed enough in my time. But take the single span arch bridge, sweeping out over a stretch of water, like a solid, grey rainbow. Beautiful. Breathtaking sight, especially in mist with the morning sun striking the brickwork. I crossed one such in Scotland...."

"Why?"

He paused in mid-stride and gave me another of his worried looks.

"Why? Because bridges are made to be crossed. They're...." He seemed to search that oversized head for the words. "They're a mystery to solve. The mystery is in the falling to Earth. The unknown revealed, for only in crossing is there discovery. Bridges are constructed for Man, by Man, to pass over the impassable — the torrent, the gorge, the wide stretch of water...."

Not entirely true. There is always a second path to the far side, albeit a slower one. However, I didn't interrupt him — it might have robbed his face of light once again.

"Bridges can be simple structures, but at the same time magnetic. They can be rope bridges shrouded in jungle steam, or — do you know Earth at all?"

I shook my head. I was from a local planet, born and bred.

"Well on Earth they have these tall mountains joined by road bridges. The Himalaya bridge is one such — *it is magnificent!*"

The words were controlled reverence. God was not, after all, the human mould but a giant bridge: a stone-steel Samson.

"Then there are those ornate structures, preserved for us by the Bridge Society, that remind us of a more fanciful age. Solid cantilevers of wrought iron. And suspension bridges, cables taut as bowstrings — a masterful show of spiderwork . . . small wooden Japanese garden bridges — for ornamentation . . . ."

Here I did interrupt.

"What about bridges that go nowhere?"

There was a short silence before he said, "Meaning what? I don't understand."

"Bridges that never fall to the ground," I said.

He gave his hand a little flick.

"There are no such things. They would be useless objects — a bridge is functional or it isn't a bridge."

"I'm not so sure. Anyway I have an idea of the function."

He chose not to listen. Instead he threw himself into an explanation of how all bridges, of whatever type, ascend and descend, or stretch an arm in some way across a natural hazard. His argument was full of flaws but I had no heart to tell him what was coming. He had, after all, a responsibility to his "group". Besides, I had my own problems. When we reached the ruins of Visilia we had approximately a month to carry out our separate tasks before the season of High Winds hit the area. (As I write *hit* I know I have chosen the correct word. The winds come suddenly, from the West, and within days reach speeds of 300 to 400 kiloms per hour. A man is a rag in the path of such winds.)

Many nights later we were still walking.

"The causeway of Othman is five miles long . . . but it never did reach the far bank."

Scaplan continued to chatter about the wonders of the bridge world when the music of the city floated through the night air and moved faintly around our ears.

"What's that?"

"Music," I replied, sardonically.

"Yes, yes. I can hear . . . but who is it? Who's playing it?"

He was worried, I think, that someone had beaten him to the Visilian bridges.

"It's the city. The place is honeycombed with windholes. It sounds pleasant now, but after a while it'll drive you mad."

"Oh, yes," he said absently, "you've been here before. . . ."

We reached the next artesian well at midnight and rested by the deep, oil-dark waters for a short while. By dawn we would be in the baked streets of the ruined city and the enigma of the Visilian population would be my constant companion once again: a phantom which remained just out of my analytical reach.

The Visilian people's disappearance amounted to one more of those deeply-buried puzzles with which archaeologists such as myself form a love-hate relationship. First I had to dig up the puzzle — then I had to unravel it. The more I became obsessed with finding an answer, the more possessive I became over the question: which of course was why I resented the intrusion of another man, even though he was a fool.

My current purpose in life was to discover who the Visilians were — or possibly *what* they were — and why they disappeared without leaving writings, artifacts (apart from ruins) or any type of skeleton. It was as if one day they simply gathered all their belongings together and went on a long march to another place. Only the incomplete shell, the city, remained. Of course, this might be exactly what did happen but I needed some circumstantial evidence. The seven-and-a-half month year with its three months of high winds didn't help me any. Also the absence of supplies on a one-man operation such as mine limited my time in the city. The reason for my being poorly-equipped, poorly-supplied and poorly-aided was simply that I was poor.

". . . and I've got a picture of a Visilian bridge," said Scaplan, as we huddled together under a makeshift shelter consisting of a reflector sheet belonging to the Earthman and some short poles we carried for the purpose. A depression had been necessary to fit us both in the shade. Scaplan's armpits, groin and feet smelled as though they were gangrenous. The air was foul and each breath torture on the lungs.

"Show it to me." I was interested.

"What for? You've seen one in the flesh ... so to speak."

"Because I'd like to see it, that's why."

He fumbled around in a breast pocket and produced a sweat-soiled clipping. It wasn't a photograph — it was a computer-assisted sketch and an unrealistic one at that. The artist was obviously a romantic with classical vision: a second- or third-hand description had produced the work, not a visit. It was a frontal view of the second bridge — I recognized the pillar insignia — and it curved upwards and across the chasm, almost to the far side. The details, of the carvings, were good. But the perspective was all wrong and it was obviously not a graphical representation but a record of the centripetal artwork of the bridge. Windblown sand had pitted and worn those flourishes but the artist depicted them as they would have originally appeared.

"You're in for a shock, Scaplan. This isn't a true...." But he had fallen asleep while I had been studying the picture. I stuffed it in his tunic and settled down myself. There is a cruel streak to my nature which I will seldom admit to. I was glad I hadn't told him. I wanted to see his face when we got to the bridges.

When we arrived at the city I took the excited Scaplan to the first of the seven bridges and on seeing it his face registered various emotions, from incomprehension, to anger, to pain. The wailing of the windholes in the towers reflected his innermost feelings and for the first time I felt a certain pity for the man.

"It doesn't reach the other side," he said finally.

I nodded. The footbridge was a single-span arch — or rather, half an arch — which swept out over the chasm like a flying buttress with no brickwork to support. It was ornate, the blocks carved out of metamorphic rock and pieced together using a type of mortar I hadn't yet been able to analyse. To either side of the bridge, lattice-work spars curved upwards out of the chasm walls like white tusks, to support the main body. There was a handrail along the top which terminated in the points of the tusks; and the lip of the bridge, where it ceased halfway across the wide abyss, sloped downward into the darkness and was smoothly finished. Clearly it was meant to halt midway.

"Surely you knew? All of them resemble this one."

"The Visilian half-bridge," he murmured. "I thought it was a structural reference — like a bascule-bridge, or a pontoon bridge. I mean — what's the *point* of such a piece of engineering?"

It was difficult to keep the glee out of my voice. "But you must have had a description — otherwise how did you know?"

His face was miserable. "The description we were given merely said there was no support from the far bank. We imagined a user merely swung himself down on to the other side — that it was maybe a few centimetres. The description wasn't that clear. 'A bridge like a horizontal waterfall' it was, 'sweeping out towards the unknown'."

"The *unknown*. Surely. . . ."

"A figure of speech. We thought . . . I *can't* disappoint them all now. I can't."

I left him there, staring down the sheer walls into the blackness below. At the bottom was hot lava. It was a fault rift, not a canyon caused by a river or glaciation. It fell a long, long way towards the heart of the world.

Later I began excavating. I had no set plan. Indiscriminate digging was as likely to produce results as well-defined trenching. Besides, I could never plan while time pressed at my back. The foundations and most of the wall areas had already been well gutted by previous better-equipped expeditions. Only the windtowers and bridges, of hard rock, remained intact. There was almost no hope of finding anything — yet I was hopeful, especially at the start of a dig. Something kept pulling me back to those streets, which were covered by soil or uncovered as the mood of the wind had it. One day, one night, I would find the first Visilian artifact and become a rich man. Better still I would be able to make calculated guesses as to their shape, or size, or origin, or final resting place . . . or maybe all four, and more. Maybe. . . .

The hot dust of the streets burned the tender insides of my nostrils and stung my eyes as I dug and sifted and carefully brushed potential finds. Scaplan sat on the left side of the bridge, staring moodily at its unusual configuration. Occasionally he shook his head and threw a pebble into the mantle's crack, probably listening for it to strike bottom.

Sometime later I noticed he was still there. I had been working feverishly amongst the scattered stones and finding nothing, resting when I was tired and gnawing on strips of pressed protein when hungry.

"Aren't you going to eat?" I called.

His shoulders were slumped forward and it was only their slow pumping movement that told me he was still alive at all.

I shrugged and carried on with my own task. Later I saw him go for water, but he returned to the same spot afterwards. He had his own rations and I supposed he was using them.

After many days his continued unmoving presence on the edge of the chasm began to irritate me. I found myself being distracted by the morose hump of his back. His very immobility seemed designed to attract my attention. I'm afraid I shouted at him: berating him close to his ear and shaking my fist in his face.

"Why don't you go?" I yelled. "There's nothing for you here . . . wasting your time, you stupid little man. I can't *afford* to worry about you. I've no time to be solicitous. . . ."

He took no notice — didn't even look at me. He just kept staring at that bridge. I cursed him again, then left him, but my digging had lost its fervour. One of the reasons I continued with my futile seasonal visits was because I enjoyed the feverish excitement they generated within me. Shifting soil can be an engrossing occupation, even though the possibility of a find is negligible. Scaplan had robbed me of my enthusiasm. I continued to search but without hope, or any real interest.

The wind came early. The low wailing began to increase in pitch and this was my warning sign. I broke away from my diggings and prepared to leave, hoping I could return alone once the High Winds had gone.

Approaching Scaplan even my insensitive nose was offended, but it was only personal hygiene, not decaying flesh.

"Are you coming?" I said. "It's dangerous to stay. Listen to those stone mouths — they're screaming at us to get the hell out and away."

He turned bright, feverish eyes on me.

"Listen, I think I've got it. Perhaps it's a trick of some kind, to keep Visilian enemies from attempting to cross. A drawbridge of sorts — only these people knew the secret of illusion. I mean the real secret. Maybe, from the other side they get an opposite picture. I'm convinced the *whole* bridge is there — it just doesn't appear that way to us . . . *A bridge always touches two sides*."

"Why don't you try it then?" I realized I was being cruel.

"I will." There was determination in his voice. "I've just got to get up my courage, that's all. Once I step out, there will be something solid beneath my feet. It's just a trick with the light. You'll see. . . ."

He really meant it. I tried to show him that he was applying human logic to an alien concept. It couldn't work. He was bending his arguments towards the conclusion he needed: a common fault amongst narrow-minded people. Reject anything which diverges from a required answer. He ignored me.

Bending down. I picked up a rock, then stepped on to the bridge, hoping that time had not weakened the supports. Scaplan gave a sort of gasp as I walked towards the middle. I wondered if it was because it appeared that I was going all the way, and was about to rob him of all his glory, or because he thought I might fall. Close to the centre the bridge sloped sharply downwards and was slippery. I gripped the rail and gently tossed the rock ahead of me. It went over the end and dropped, uninterrupted, to the lava deep below. I walked back to Scaplan.

He turned moody eyes on me.

"Doesn't mean a thing," he said. "I've tried things like that. The Visilians weren't fools — they'd know an enemy would test such things and build in safeguards. More illusions or something."

"What?" I shouted, angrily.

"I don't know. I'm not a Visilian."

The wind was growing in strength and I tried to pull him to his feet. He pushed me off roughly.

"Damn you then," I replied, and set off quickly in the direction of the desert.

I looked back once at his distant figure, still hunched over the abyss. The wind was howling around me like a savage dog, snatching at my clothes and tearing at the exposed areas of my skin with abrasive gritty teeth.

I hurried on.

Barely making it to shelter before the fury reached its climax, my situation had given me little time for feelings of guilt. However, once out of the oasis and inside the banyan building, I began to experience remorse at having left Scaplan to certain death. I informed the authorities of course, and a rescue team reluctantly left the safety of the oasis in a heavy, enclosed half-track to search for him. They returned some hours later empty-handed. The sand had thickened the air until visibility was virtually zero. It was a hopeless task to find the city, let alone Scaplan. Either he had choked to death on dust by now — or he had walked along his bridge and out into space. *A bridge always touches two sides*. I began drinking.

Scaplan's suburban logic wound its way through my brain as I integrated his arguments with my own opinions on the fate of the Visilians. Possibly he had been right, though I doubted he would recognize the answer. The disappearance of a nation can have many causes, both swift and slow. Plague, migration, war, pestilence, but one word stuck to my mind. *Religion*.

Just as an exercise in my own logic I considered the emergence of a new religion which promised a better deal from life than suffering hot dust and high winds. A suicide cult aligned with the promise of cool fountains and calm skies in the afterlife. A short walk to happiness.

Other arguments were as feasible: a migratory people that moved, say, after each generation of young had been raised? That would give them time to build a solid city. The bridges could have been quays from which they, as winged creatures perhaps, could launch themselves out on to the thermals created by the lava pools below.

Or maybe the bridges were sacrificial platforms? The tools and other artifacts mostly fashioned from materials that corroded, finally to become dust?

Possibly there was a disease and the bodies and belongings had been thrown into the chasm in an attempt to halt an epidemic? A ceremonial garbage tip?

These were vague improbabilities, but the one I liked the best was the suicide cult. It fitted neatly with my picture of the

Visilians as a "damn you to hell, you bastard world" race. A perverse group of beings — as stubborn as Scaplan.

As I drank I pictured the figure of Scaplan waiting at the foot of the bridge — afraid to go on, yet equally determined not to go back. A man trapped by his dilemma into doing nothing while the agent of his death increased in fury around him. The scene was printed indelibly on my mind, like the blue lines of the figures near the bridge on a willow-patterned plate. I could never go back now, because he'd still be sitting alongside that damned half-arch which had killed him — either directly or indirectly. I would not be able to work with those pebble eyes on my back night and day: the gnome-like figure full of accusations as I scraped away at the soil.

How could I have saved him? I don't know — anything that suggests itself to me now seems impractical. I wish I had saved him. Not for his sake, but for mine. Scaplan could have killed himself a dozen times over and I wouldn't have cared, but not at Visilia. At the time I was interested only in my own survival but I wish now I had concerned myself with him as well. Perhaps if I'd been more sympathetic in the beginning when he learned about the bridge — or tried to take his mind off the problem in some way. Maybe if I'd attempted to interest him in my work, he might have climbed out of his depression. Instead he dug himself deeper until he couldn't pull himself out.

I wish I could have stopped him from committing suicide in *my* city. Now his mundane, vulgar ghost mingles with the spirits of my exotic lost aliens, walks their streets and moans through the windholes of their towers.

I can never go back. Scaplan has defiled my city, damn his soul to hell.

THE INVISIBLE FOE

"Shadow and sunlight are the same —
and one to me are shame and fame."
"Brahma" by Ralph Waldo Emerson

Singapore, my adopted city, moved slowly into the path of the day's first rays of sunshine. It was monsoon season, and the humidity was high: a day of wet sunlight.

Street cleaners were about, pushing their boxwood handcarts towards littered destinations to brush away the debris of a night-time explosion of people. Walking along Boogey Street, I waved to several transsexuals and transvestites still occupying roadside tables. The *Kai Tai:* female hormones gave many of them a complexion and surface beauty even more beguiling than women. It was not uncommon for merchant seamen looking for whores to make a mistake. Such a beautiful people anyway — a blending of several Eastern cultures. I had an affinity with the *Kai Tai* because we held similar secrets: we seemed what we were not. We both hid beneath layers of untruth: the *Kai Tai* under the guise of women, and myself . . . my pretence was that of being human.

One of them nodded as I passed.

"Morning Thin Chai," he said.

"Morning Lucy," I smiled. I kept my voice soft. The night people were not rowdy or coarse. It was the long-noses that created all the noise. They drank heavily, shouted through mouthfuls of prawns, were sick where they stood and shattered the street air with their shrieks and raucous laughter. Jansen was a *Wai Lo:* an Occidental. Perhaps that was why my mouth tasted of snake bile? I was on my way to meet him, in a subordinate role. That a *Wai Lo*, a *ghost person*, should consider himself my superior filled me with shame.

Japanese motorbikes growled somewhere beyond a row of shops. A proprietor dozing on his raffia bed, on the porch of his premises, stirred and scratched himself through his dirty vest.

The city was beginning to wake.

(I had been there the previous evening, a girl with oranges on her breath at my side. We had sat away from the hanging lanterns, in the shadows, and watched the swift process of change — the metamorphosis of money into gutter filth. I felt no revulsion, merely a detached interest in folly. I was a student of the art, if it is such, and not a science as Jansen would have it. Whatever the category, the study of weakness can only reward infiltrators like myself. It is useful to turn a vice inwards, on its creator, like a dagger.

When the evening's subjects had staggered away along the drunkard's walk, Nancy Ho followed me to my room. In the bareness of my small apartment she nestled against my narrow body.

There were cracks on the wall into which the house lizards wriggled. Her body was silken to the touch. Insects rustled through folds in paper curtains. Dry, shadow-thin sighs escaped my lips. On the card-thin weatherboard, a cockroach scratched its path across the shoulder of the house. Afterwards, I had to open the shutters to let the hot room breathe its odours out into the night, then stroked her hair till we fell asleep.)

By the time I reached the dockside the streets were flowing with vehicles and people. I was pleased with myself for I had not once looked towards Li Hoe Hill and my ugly creation, which adorned its brow like the despised crown of a despot. Though its white columns were printed indelibly upon the cornea of my mind's eye, I could lie to myself, so long as I did not confirm its existence. Perhaps the night rain had washed it away? Perhaps a giant dragon had swallowed it in the rays of the previous evening's dying sun? Perhaps it had vanished, the victim of magic conjured up by the geomancer who hated its presence more than he feared death?

He was standing by a capstan, overdressed in a dark European suit. It could only be Jansen, correctness extending into stupidity. The white Panama hat was his only obvious concession to the heat, but it looked incongruous on his narrow head and he snatched it off the moment he saw me. Was it possible he could read my thoughts? More probably it was the expression on my face. My feelings refuse to remain submerged and surface quickly.

"Chai?" he said, his tone unsure. "You've lost weight."

"A little," I replied.

He extended a hand. I shook it and he passed me his hat with his other hand, as if it was the most natural thing in the world that I should accept an inferior role. I was his lackey: a carrier of hats. No doubt he would soon pass me his jacket.

"No suitcases?" I queried.

He shook his head. "Not necessary. I'm flying to London tonight. I've asked the people on the boat to send my luggage directly to the airport."

Jansen had come from Australia by ship. No doubt the people on the boat had served him royally, and I was expected to carry on the tradition.

He rubbed the fingertips of his left hand against his palm and frowned. It was a peculiar gesture, but I made an attempt at an interpretation.

"Yes, the air has a texture to it here. It's the humidity. You'll be wet through if you continue to keep that coat on."

"No, no," he said, a faintly irritated tone to his voice. "It's that heavy smell. It's almost tangible. I swear it's entering my pores."

Normally unaware of what was always part of my life, I tried to tune in to the odours around me. Fish? Cooked rice? Squid? There was nothing unsavoury that I could recognize. Shrugging my shoulders, I led the way from the docks into the streets. There was noise now, but it was of business.

Jansen stood with an appalled look on his face as powerful waves of humanity flowed past him in the street. The scene had an atmosphere of quiet panic, as if a series of crises were about to occur in specific locations and people were moving swiftly from one safe area to another.

"I thought you said you had it all wrapped up." His voice was angry. "Did you bring me all the way to see this? You said . . ."

I interrupted him. "I told you the truth. Wait. I'll show you." I thrust his hat back into his hands and he seemed surprised. "Put that on. You'll need it. And please — take off the jacket and tie. You draw attention to yourself."

"Are we *walking?*" he said incredulously, as I strolled ahead.

"It's quicker," I called over my shoulder. "We're going through the back streets. Even the trishaws find it too narrow."

When he caught me up I saw that he was in his shirt-sleeves, his coat over his arm. I smiled to myself. Was it possible that we came from the same loins? This arrogant, pompous fool and myself? How long ago lay the fork in time when we took our different paths, he to Europe and I to the Far East? By our differences it must have been a millennium — and yet I knew it was only ten years. Before that we were as alike in spirit as identical twins, my anarchist brother and I.

Before I was allowed to adopt human form my tutors in cultural sabotage insisted that I absorb much of Chinese history. Authenticity of character, I was told, was essential if we were to oust these upstarts, these usurpers of our ancient Earth. My studies included old stories; half truth, half lie, such as I was to become, indivisible, fused into a single entity.

There is a Chinese legend which I found I could compare with our fall from grace.

In the days of the early knights, two famous warriors met to do single combat. Instead of crossing blades they stood apart, their faces like stone, and studied each other for physical flaws, for weaknesses in spirit.

Psychological combat.

For three days they stood in tense concentration. On the morning of the fourth, one of the knights had gone. Only his sword remained in the ground, a symbol of his shame. The battle had been won and lost without the need for blows. Each knew of the other, had studied his history — his skills, moods, weaponry, strength, stamina, tactics — all those intricate and intimate ingredients which go to make the warrior. Like chess players, they each assessed the other's potential, gauged reactions to every possible move and countermove. "If I should do this, he will counter thus," or thus, or thus ... and so each physical action, each emotional reaction is considered until the final realization of who has lost and who has won.

So it was between the humans and ourselves over possession of the Earth. We lost that mental combat, at the beginning of time, and later had to disappear into remote retreats in woodlands, mountains, and wastelands. Now we are few, but emerging once

again. Seeking our revenge. Our ancestors had come, peacefully,
from a distant, dying world, beyond the curve of Orion's belt, at a
time when our science was accepted as magic. We were called
witches and wizards but though we have the ability to change our
physical appearance it *is* a *science*, not an art.

We took a short cut through a park full of businessmen in their
shirt-sleeves. In slow motion they practised the martial art of *Tai
Chi Chuen* on invisible opponents. The exercise was mentally and
physically rewarding without producing fatigue. Jansen watched
their movements with an enraged look on his face. Then he
muttered, "Bloody fairies," and scowled at the nearest of them, as
if they posed a threat to his future plans for Singapore.

   Someone spoke in Cantonese as I passed, looking quizzically
at Jansen as she did so. I murmured back.

   "Who's that?" asked my brother. Wary lines had appeared
upon his sallow features.

   "A friend's sister. Don't be concerned."

   "What did she say?" He was hurrying alongside me, trying to
weave as I did through the crowds, but not having a great deal of
success.

   "She said: 'Hello, Thin Chai'," I replied patiently. "What's
wrong? Are you expecting someone to spring out and accuse us
of being anarchists?"

   "I thought," he said suspiciously, "your surname was Chai.
Why would a friend call you by your surname?"

   "Because she's Chinese — we always use family names."

   "Why?"

   "Why not? It's the custom. If it's a big family, like Wong or
Lee, we add a little description, like Fat Wong or Tall Wong. It
becomes part of the name. Within the family we call each other
First Brother or Second Sister — depending upon age."

   "Don't they have Christian names?"

   "Some of us do — if we're Christian. Some of us just have
second or third names." I wanted to confuse him. Since living in
Singapore I have developed a simple, effective weapon which I
normally use against that ugly invader, the *Wai Lo* long-nose. I
told the plain truth, without adding any explanation. "Like
Lucy *Lee* Man Lo. He's a close friend, but I call him Lucy

because he's a Christian."

"Lucy?" His sweating face wore a puzzled expression, but he did not question further. He took off his hat and fanned himself as he walked. "Why do you keep saying *we* and *us?*" he complained. "You talk as if you were one of them. I hope there's something to show me."

There was an undisguised threat in his voice, and I nodded knowingly.

"Yes, First Brother," I replied, sweetly. "Of course there is."

We found our way into the back streets of the tenement buildings. Bamboo poles covered in laundry protruded from each window sill up to the sky. Every day is a white flag day in Singapore. There was rubbish flowing sluggishly down the gutters which would disappear with the four o'clock monsoon downpour. The streets were greasy, and Jansen continually slipped in his leather-soled sandals. A woman passed in a Choeng Sam with a slit to the thigh.

"Don't stare," I warned him as his eyes strayed. "Chinese don't like it and they have quick tempers."

I received an answering grunt, but nothing more.

"The *noise*," he grumbled, a little while later. I had to admit the level was rather high, even for this section of the town. Carpenters, panel beaters, ironsmiths, and a dozen other trades waged battles of sound with infants and babies. Nobody shuts their windows in the back streets. Who wants to stifle?

"There's one," I pointed to an empty tenement flat. "Another two further on."

He took hold of my arm to stop me walking on and produced a handkerchief to wipe his face and neck.

"One?" he said. "One? What the hell is this? I thought you had things in hand. A handful of empty flats isn't what I expected."

I said mildly, "You do realize that we had a tremendous over-crowding problem? Hundreds were sleeping in the streets."

"So?"

"So most of the homeless have left — not only that, several of those who *did* have homes have gone. In the residential areas the vacancy count is much higher, but I thought this would impress you more. These people can't afford to leave — but they *are* leaving."

"Hmm. Well, I still have to be convinced. This operation has to be finely tuned. It has to get its timing right to fall in step with the rest of the scheme. Otherwise . . ."

"Let's face it, Jansen," I replied, "Singapore is one of the least important areas. It hardly matters at all . . ."

"Every area matters," he interrupted. "Get things into perspective. We want to hit every part of them — if Singapore is the little finger of that ugly sprawling body called humanity, then crush it."

I acknowledged his concern, but assured him that everything was under control. After living ten years among these people I knew their attitudes and beliefs like my own. I was sure of my timing. Of course there was an element of guesswork, but I felt that clever statistical planning had narrowed a wide chance to a near certainty. As every gambler knows, there is six times the chance of 7 appearing from a roll of the dice than there is of 2 coming up. I always planned for the appearance of a 7.

"Where will they go?" he asked. "These people?"

"Some of them will move to the countryside — which can't possibly support them. The others to already overcrowded areas, like Changi. There, living will become difficult. Of course we won't clear the city completely — but to all intents and purposes it will be depopulated. They rely on this great, noisy animal to keep their economy at the level it is — which isn't terribly high. If people leave the city in great numbers it will weaken the island as a whole."

"Good, good. That's all I ask for." He gave my arm a fraternal squeeze. "I just want to be sure it'll work, that's all. I think I trust you, Chai. . . ."

He made an attempt at humour, which was for him a great effort. ". . . You're my, let's see, my seven-hundredth brother. Give or take a few. We're quite close really, when you put a number to it."

"I think it's more than that," I said, "but I'm flattered by your show of affection. Shall we go now? To see the casino?"

He stuffed the handkerchief into his pocket and tipped the ridiculous-looking Panama on to the back of his head.

"Ah yes, the casino," he said. "I'm looking forward to that. Is that it? Up there on the hill?"

The Chinese in me flooded my soul with shame. I stared past his shoulder into a doorway where some children played. One of them looked up at me and smiled.

"Yes," I said. "On the hill."

Smile at the traitor, child, for he is not really a traitor — not one of your own kind — but a creature of another race. I DO NOT TRESPASS ON THIS EARTH. This is my world as much as it is yours. Smile, child, smile at the saboteur. Yes, yes, traitor too then, for if I feel such, then I am.

"What's the matter with you? Are you ill?" Jansen asked.

"No, not ill. Weary."

"Are we going or not?"

"By the way," I said, walking away. "This is your year in the Chinese calender."

His clownish features broke into a grin. He caught up with me.

"Really? You mean my lucky year — astrologically? You don't believe in that rubbish, do you? You've been here too long, Chai."

"No, not really. I just thought it would interest you."

It was the year of the monkey. It was not to do with stars but with caricatures.

We took a taxi to Li Hoe Hill. The driver used the horn as if it had some magical arrangement with the laws of nature which would lift up the vehicle and float it over the crowded streets.

"What's the name of this device you are using? I know you informed me in your last report, but I've forgotten. I have so much to remember."

"*Fung Shui*. Not so much a device — more a set of beliefs. The art of adapting the residence of the living — and the dead — so as to co-operate and harmonize with the local currents of cosmic breath."

He nodded, settling back in the Mercedes.

"If I've got it right, when a man wishes to build a house he calls in an expert in *Fung Shui*?"

"A geomancer. The builders or designers will be told by him which way to face the structure to ensure the best fortune for the occupants. *Fung Shui* extends to many other aspects of life and death . . . even one's grave."

"I see." It was not a commitment to the idea. Merely an acknowledgment that the concept was worth considering. Jansen reserved his judgment, as would most Western Europeans, on Oriental "magic". I, in my Chinese role, was of course very sympathetic to the belief, without allowing myself total commitment.

"It's not merely hocus-pocus, you know. It has a certain factual basis — the best position for sunlight — in sight of water. *Fung Shui* means literally 'wind and water' in Cantonese . . . also the geomancer uses a compass to determine the Earth's magnetic field." Geomantic compasses were instruments set in old baked clay discs and inscribed with concentric circles, I added, after a pause.

"So?"

"So who's to say that if one lives in the flow of the field it's not beneficial? Physically, spiritually, and mentally. They may consider the field to be represented by some mythical, invisible dragon, but that doesn't cancel any probable real benefits."

"True, but I wouldn't use the word *probable*. It would take a lot to convince me of any underlying fact in the belief. However," he conceded, "I am willing to admit that the mind is a very powerful instrument, able to produce effect without cause — especially in the individual. But I'm not as certain as you are that this belief in *Fung Shui* is so deep-rooted, in a general, racial sense. Perhaps some of them just prefer to play safe, and when it comes to a choice between staying in the city where they have a certain security or moving elsewhere and raising the risk of survival — well, that may be a different matter."

"Look, let me try to explain. We're not dealing with logic — at least, not with European logic. *Fung Shui* deals with the relationships of objects to one another, as well as nature. A new building will disturb the already-established *Fung Shui* of its environment. The garden shaped like a sword will pierce the heart of a neighbouring house. Bad luck is almost always attributed to a discordant *Fung Shui* — even if the causes are not obvious. . . ."

"So a geomancer's some kind of priest?"

He had surprised me. There *was* a subtle mechanism at work beneath his skull after all.

"That's a keen observation," I replied. "Not strictly accurate ... but near enough."

I sensed he was waiting for me to try to convince him. Then he could attack my insubstantial arguments and prove to me how foolish I was. I let the logician simmer in his own concrete thoughts as we climbed up the back of the dragon, past the bars outside which sat perennial mah-jong players.

Sparrows. The four winds. Dragons. Beauty was everywhere in our land; even gambling was dressed in graceful words. My friends, the various races of Singapore, would appreciate my skill, if not my motives, in bringing bad fortune to the land. I was the unhuman anarchist in human form. The unseen enemy. The subtle fifth-columnist. I was here to erode their society, to destroy them from within. We are few and they are many ... but still I find it distasteful. I know what prompted my superiors to place me in a minor role. I was too willing a pupil, too eager to learn human ways. Not know thy enemy but *become* thy enemy. Jansen has remained unchanged. I am ... impressionable. Pressed into my soul is the seal of Thin Chai. Where does Thin Chai end? Where do the old ways begin?

"Is that it?" said Jansen, as we rounded the last curve.

I tapped the taxi driver on the shoulder. "Stop here," I ordered. Jansen and I got out and walked a few yards to the shade of a palm.

"You spoke to him in English. Why?" asked my brother, when we were out of earshot. "He was Chinese, like you."

"You really are the most —"

"I have to be careful. Please answer the question."

I was irritated. We were both on trust, Jansen as much as I was.

"He doesn't speak my dialect," I replied. "He's from the Malay Peninsula — they use Hok Yen there. I was only taught Cantonese ... what would you have me do? Speak all the languages of Earth? That wouldn't attract attention at all, would it?"

"Cut the sarcasm. Okay, let's forget it. I'm ... sorry. Now, this is the casino?"

"Yes." I was still not completely mollified and kept the edge to my voice.

"It looks rather splendid to me," said Jansen, obviously trying to view the monstrosity through my eyes.

"The facade is mock Grecian," I replied.

"Yes?"

"This is the Orient. It's as out of place as an . . . it's *alien*, if you'll forgive the expression."

"Of course it is, but aren't they all?" he said with humour.

"It's also a patchwork of classic styles. Those columns are a mixture of Corinthian, Doric, and Ionic. It's tasteless; and to use one of your own terms, it's kitsch. Finally, it's as big and white as an albino whale, and on this hill can be seen from every corner of the city. The sun catches this ugly beast and blinds the eyes of all those who are forced to look up at its offensive marble pillars."

"But that's not all, is it? There is also . . . *Fung Shui*?"

"Ah, yes," I said, sadly, almost hiding my face in my hands with shame. "*Fung Shui*."

"You had the geomancer divine . . . if that's the right expression, divine the correct position and direction for our Grecian casino and then deliberately . . ."

"I had it built so that it faced the wrong way. The position is all wrong. It's the manifestation of bad luck . . . unavoidable because it dominates the whole city." It was a symbol of dissonance and it permeated the lives of all those who lived and worked within the sight of this alien folly.

"At night it's so well lit with spotlights you can see it from the ships in the harbour."

"I wish I'd known," Jansen said. "I'd have gone on deck specially to look. Why the high fence and the men with pickaxe handles? Having trouble with some of your punters trying to get their money back?"

I shook my head.

"Arson. Someone has tried to burn it down twice but it's nothing to do with the gambling . . ."

"Bad *Fung Shui*? Some people from the city below? That's a good sign, Chai. It means they must hate it badly enough to risk jail."

"I know."

I looked back at the taxi. The driver had averted his face, was looking out over the sweltering city, towards the sea. Was it a subconscious act? My design had been to manipulate the sixth sense: a subliminal erosion of confidence and the implantation of unease. He would see any hill, however small, as a dragon, and buildings erected on sensitive parts of the beast as abhorrent to the natural order of forms. The casino was built on the dragon's tail, thus bringing disharmony to his world. When we rose against them they would be weakened, both mentally and spiritually.

Jansen said, "And they're leaving because of this?"

"Beginning to. Most of them probably won't admit to why they are going ... but they'll follow a strong instinct. When things begin to sour you look for an excuse, somewhere to lay the blame. Gradually they'll drift away, those who feel its influence most strongly. And others will follow. Even those who scoff at *Fung Shui*, or do not have the same beliefs will eventually leave. Who wants to live in a dying city?"

"Well, I hope it works. We have our job to do ... our preparations. I expect it cost the Earth ... does anyone suspect you?"

"Don't concern yourself on my part — I employed foreign contractors through a European agent. I wouldn't want my friends to think I was responsible for *this*."

Many bribes had changed hands too, but I was safe. My contact with officials and authorities was buffered by several people no longer on the island.

"I wasn't concerned for you. Just for our presence."

Our presence. We had to weaken the system without arousing suspicion. Subtle, devious ways. The neuroses of the West were easy to handle; and Jansen, as the co-ordinator, was having great successes there. In the East, where there were few strong economies, less stable governments, a smaller task faced us. In Singapore, I alone was responsible. Once we felt the humans were weak enough, over the whole Earth, then the uprising would take place. We would gather in pre-appointed places and cut through the rotten flanks of humanity like red-hot scythes. Then we would turn on them, left and right, and slaughter them as they had done us.

That was the plan, but of course to succeed it needed organization. We were normally so poor at co-ordination and unity. Jansen — or Ertois as he had been born — had the gift of organization. We relied on him to pull it all together, produce a feasible plan which would ensure victory despite the disparity in numerical strengths. Our weapons, the earth movements, quakes, eruptions, were as destructive as their missiles. But we needed Jansen's genius to make it all work. Being egocentric, he carried the plan in his head, so none of the glory could be taken from him. He was our General — or, as he preferred to be called, The Co-ordinator. Ten years ago he had disclosed the gist of his plans and we began to put them into effect. *Demoralize the enemy, then strike.*

As we stood and stared at the building I caught sight of a little man, standing by the corner of the fence. He was watching us intently. I knew him. We shared a common name. Chai. The Chais proliferate — there were many so called. One can get lost in a name, I thought.

"I want this to work," said Jansen, close to my ear. "I don't want anything to go wrong. Not at this stage."

"Of course not," I said without conviction. "That would be disastrous. We anarchists have a holy duty to perform — God knows."

I almost disclosed my closest secret then. He was my brother, after all, in a different life.

He said, "You know our task, Chai. You know what we must do to undermine their society. In the West I have child psychologists and economists using their expertise to guide humanity down paths leading to self-destruction ... here, you must turn their culture inside-out to bring them to ruin." He tried to justify our position. "We didn't come to Earth from Mocte seeking this war. It's been thrust upon us by centuries of persecution."

"What persecution?"

He glared at me. "We have to live with these ugly bodies, don't we? We have to conform to their ways, their thinking, their damned ... look, look, I don't like being repressed, Chai. Let *them* go into hiding for a few hundred years. Let us have a taste of the power."

"You talk about our forefathers, but who are *we*, Jansen? What are we — to ourselves, our human selves?"

He laughed. "To the humans? We are all the ghosts of lonely roads, all the tales of supernatural woodland, moor, and cave. The footprints in the mountain snows. The small religions of remote tribes. We are the stories that end, 'Who's there?' and never give an answer. The listeners. The watchers."

"But are we?" I insisted. "I've forgotten what I am."

"We might be — perhaps once in a thousand times it is us — the invisible foe. You know," he was obviously in a reflective mood, "sometimes I wonder. Sometimes I ask myself: do we need to do this to them? If we showed ourselves, in our natural forms, wouldn't they accept us? Perhaps even like us?"

My heart was racing within my chest.

"And what do you answer?"

He fixed his eyes on me, and his reply destroyed any hopes that he had raised by his previous words.

"I remember how much I hate them."

Just after four o'clock the rains came: a flood of warm water which brought out the waxpaper umbrellas and, afterwards, the bullfrogs. Much later I took Jansen to Boogey Street, just as it was beginning to unfold. He was fond of red-light districts and talked enthusiastically about the Gut in Malta, the Reeperbahn, Soho, and many others of which I had never heard.

We reached a hand-painted sign which read "Drinks at Logical Prices" — a direct translation from the Chinese.

"What's that noise?" he asked, as we entered the Jungle Club, the small bar where I occasionally met my friends.

"What noise?"

"That . . . clicking."

I listened. "Oh! Chit-Chats. House lizards . . . overhead, they're all over the ceiling."

He looked up and shuddered.

"Frogs. Lizards. Bats. This place . . ." He shook himself again. "I've sweated buckets and the whole place stinks of overcooked food and heavy perfume. How can you live here?"

"I have to . . . remember?"

"Hmmm . . ."

A deep, husky voice said, "Hello . . . who this fine man you brought, Thin Chai?"

We turned together. Lucy was sitting at a small table in the corner in a dress which revealed a great deal of silicone cleavage. He smiled at us and blew a ring of smoke through painted lips.

I introduced them and went away to buy the drinks. By the time I returned Jansen had his hand on Lucy's knee. It was almost . . . domestic. Although we had only adopted human form, with that form went a whole range of emotions and desires. We were as weak, or as strong, as any of our potential enemies. Our affection for individuals ran as deep as theirs: our affiliations and loyalties too. Wherein lay the question of betrayal? And to whom? Was I Thin Chai? Or was I someone else, of whom I had only dim memories? Memories which rebelled at being forced past a point some ten years in the past? Would it make any difference if I ordered the destruction of the casino — tonight, or perhaps tomorrow? I knew it would not make the slightest difference. My local friends would still be violated and I would be removed. There remained a question: who was the betrayer and who was the betrayed?

If there had been a coexistence of two souls I could not now recognize a division. My human shape was created — I was not implanted within one. I was not a parasite. I was both the betrayer and the betrayed. Jansen might easily come to terms with a callous dismissal of Asia, but how did he feel about his own part of the world? The country which he had called his own for the past ten years?

Paradox. Schizophrenia. Genuine madness. I had lived with them for a decade, these wraiths that pulled my loyalties in opposite directions. Perhaps we were insane, Jansen and I, and the world was really safe, except from a conspiracy of lunatics playing insidious games.

"What are you staring at?" he said.

My thoughts evaporated under his scowl. There was no battle of spirits raging within Jansen. His souls were models of compatibility: both were forged from a sense of duty.

"You like Lucy?" I asked. He had obviously forgotten our conversation earlier in the day, which was a symptom of his habit of retaining only that which he considered important.

"She's a nice girl," said Jansen, reluctantly withdrawing his hand as I sat down and handed round the drinks.

"Of course she is," I smiled at Lucy. "There's more warmth in Lucy than a brigade of Europeans." Lucy wrinkled his nose at me.

"You bad man, Thin Chai. You never bring me any boyfren'. This man say he go home in one half-hour."

If he doesn't, he'll get the shock of his life. His indoctrination did not include the crossing of heterosexual boundaries.

"Here's to Singapore," said Jansen, suddenly, raising his glass. "What is it . . . the *Lion City*."

"The Lion City," I murmured. Lucy and I clicked glasses with him. The nocturnal noises of Boogey Street were as lively as ever. I sipped slowly at my drink, trying to hide my sadness in the small glass. A disease was slowly killing the city and all that I held important was dying with it . . . the very least of which was me. There was something to do.

"Excuse me," I said. "I'll call the taxi. If you could follow me outside, in about two minutes . . ."

Jansen nodded, curtly, then smiled at Lucy.

"He's a good man," he said.

I left them and went out into the street. I stood for a moment, absorbing the scene around me. Stall owners were preparing for the onslaught of long-noses, hanging squid from hooks and arranging duck's eggs in neat piles with ovolo walls. Their lanterns bobbed on the evening breeze.

The night pressed around me. In the last few minutes I had made a decision but I could not be the one. My instrument was standing at the entrance to an alley. He had been following me for many weeks now, suspicious, watching, waiting. A small man. Chai Leung, a geomancer. The agents for the casino had rejected his advice. He was a man mortally wounded by shame and I knew that he carried a slim blade next to his vengeful heart. I crossed the street and joined him in the shadows.

"He's coming," I said, "the man who employed the agents." The lie slipped easily from my lips.

The geomancer's eyes met mine. He studied me for a moment, then his stare returned to the doorway through which Jansen would emerge.

"In the spleen," I advised, softly. They . . . we are not immortal.

We are as vulnerable as the form we employ.

I could not kill him. He was my brother. Of the old people, Jansen, as the co-ordinator, was the only one who knew my human face. The art of invisibility is to blend. In the backstreets we melt into one another. There are few names to share among many: Chai, Cheung, Wong, Chan. I could disappear into my adopted name forever. The main point was: I did not care. My cause had been reversed. Inside-out.

Jansen would not even see the geomancer — as assassins Chinese have few equals. We . . . they are the invisible foe. I heard his loud laugh coming from the bar and began to walk away, to be out of sight.

As I walked away, I noticed the geomancer make a sign with his left hand. Someone at the window above me moved quickly. I had underestimated both Chai Leung and *Fung Shui*. Bad fortune is often the scapegoat for a dozen other ills. Incompetence and inefficiency are two of the prime causes for the failure of a business, but what small tradesman believes a lack of success is his own fault? The hand signals passed swiftly, silently, up and down the walkways. By the time I turned the corner of Boogey Street there were at least thirty figures waiting with the geomancer, standing in doorways and alleys. Poor Jansen, he would see them after all as they fell on him in their tens, each hoping his blade would erase the bad luck. The longer he stayed inside, the more there would be.

Tomorrow we would start the demolition.

ALMOST HEAVEN

... and we came to a low, wide valley with cool terraces covered in fists of fruit trees. Through the middle of the valley ran a green, clear river into which we fell in dusty hundreds, bathing and drinking, and for the first time in many months, laughing. The pack animals, too, clustered at the water's edge taking in long draughts of liquid and bellowing their delight. The great march over the Eastern Deserts was over, and we had found the interior.

As one of the forward scouts I was first upon the town. On glimpsing the white walls of the houses through the evergreen, I felt a certain disappointment, which was foolish really, since the slopes had obviously been cultivated: we were not the first. There was a strange feeling of trespassing as we walked cautiously through the weed-covered empty streets. Silence is not a comfortable companion in alien surroundings. We called out, once or twice, thinking they might be hiding from us — half-expecting that they would fall upon us with primitive weapons, since we were surely the first humans to reach the valley. By the time we found the central building, with its huge pear-shaped bell, we were reasonably sure they had gone — either temporarily, or perhaps permanently.

"Ghost town," said Baker, but his blue eyes kept flicking along the rooftops. Finally, after inspecting most of the dwellings, we allowed the others to enter. Night fell and we posted sentries. Some camped in the streets rather than violate the dwellings. I watched the domestic stock incessantly. If there were any hostile aliens, the first signs of nervousness would come from the animals. Our watch fires picked out only shadows, and by dawn confidence had grown. Though wary, we were still hard from the privations of the journey, and our weapons, we knew, would be superior to any *they* would use. We had not at that time shed our colonial arrogance and still carried, banner-like, the bigot's belief in a unique righteousness. We saw it our duty to impose our culture, not to blend it with another.

I had a friend, ugly as the trunk of an olive tree. Her name was Theloniki. Baker, Thel and I were the best scouts: we were most suited to the work, having those qualities necessary to ensure the smoothest passage for the caravan. We were natural navigators; were not oblivious to caution yet had an underlying professional sense of adventure. Since Atkins went missing, Baker had preferred to work alone. Thel and I never let each other get beyond communicating distance — whether it was sight or sound. I was the youngest, at twenty-seven years. Thel was nearly twice my age. Baker fell somewhere between us. That any of us should be less important than we had been, or would ever be regarded as interesting but obsolete characters of best-forgotten times had crossed our minds fleetingly, if at all. We had been too busy reaching for the next horizon. Our fall was sudden. We might as well have joined Atkins in his ravine, or wherever it was that his body lay. Within a week the people had moved into the empty houses and had begun to regulate their domesticity. They no longer needed scouts. The requirement was for tradesmen, farmers and herdsmen — yes, and artists too, for there was time for appreciation once more. It was a time for leisure and crafts. But not for wandering. People had had enough of new hills, fresh plains, wide deserts. They wanted to rest their legs and exercise their arms.

I have seen holograms in the old First City which my parents colonized: three-dimensional pictures of towns pocketed by hillsides on faraway Earth. Hills around a sea called the Mediterranean. This alien-built town was similarly fashioned, with low houses fitting into the natural hollows of the rock and interconnected by a maze of winding alleys, steps and narrow streets. From a long way off it appeared as a single amorphous, nebulous construction. I loved it at first sight. It was white, cool and purpose-built.

We were sitting outside the place we shared, Thel, Baker and I, watching the sun pulling in its evening nets. I think all three of us wished we were caught in those shining meshes, and were being dragged happily to the unknown regions beyond the valley.

"Must have been dwarfs," muttered Baker, taking a pinch of snuff and snorting a period to his speech.

"Like Ganty here," smiled Thel, her face gathering more wrinkles than the neck of a tortoise.

I shrugged, huffily. They always made fun of my small stature when we were passing idle time. Just the way Baker and I teased Thel about her features. Thel and I never laughed at Baker though. He didn't invite humour.

"Smaller than Ganty," said Baker, thoughtfully.

"If such a thing was possible," added Thel, with less generosity.

We were speaking of the aliens that had once owned the town. Their single-storied buildings had ceilings high enough for our tallest people, but the entrances were squat and wide. They had left furniture of a sort which suggested their anatomic proportions fell into line with the shape of the doorways: large concave stools and circular wooden couches worn smooth with use.

"Why'd they leave, do you think?" I asked for the tenth time.

Thel replied, "Maybe they'll be back. Though I doubt it. Those slopes are at least a year overgrown. There'll be no crop this season and the pruning's late."

"You talk like a farmer," I muttered.

"I *was* a farmer," snapped Thel, "before. Didn't like it," she added with some asperity.

So there we were, the town was a gift from an unknown race. Unknown to us, that is. We had a fertile valley, more than adequate for our needs — it gave our population stretching space for several generations — and a good growing climate. It was as close to heaven as most of us wanted — Thel, Baker and me excluded of course. The town was a bonus, albeit a suspicious one. We knew about Greek wooden horses but this didn't seem to fit the case. There was nothing the aliens could possibly want that we would have, except ourselves. After the accident with the bell, which was not really an accident at all, we began to get an insight to the culture of the town's previous occupants.

On the journey I had courted a girl called Sally. She was the daughter of a cooper, whose barrel-making was obviously not a sought-after skill while we were crossing deserts and mountains. Once in the valley however, his services were very much in need; and whereas my own standing in the community was somewhat diminished, Sally's father had grown in status. The consequence of this was, he encouraged another of Sally's beaus — a carpenter named John Fennick — and my own nose was unwelcome past the doorjamb of Sally's new home. It was not that the cooper didn't like me. It was just that my prospects were zero-rated.

Naturally this turn in my fortunes — totally unexpected — was irksome to me. I tried to see Sally secretly, but it seemed that the gilt was peeling from my image. She was more interested in carpentry than tales of lone pathfinding. Thel told me I was lucky.

"You've got a head on your shoulders boy. That girl's got mincemeat between her ears. She'd have driven you starin' within a year. Find someone with brains in her head, not in her sewin' hand."

"Someone with a face like a Thai monkey?" I retorted cruelly, more out of embarrassment and chagrin than malice.

"Someone about three feet high," she retaliated, not in the least offended.

I took my horse and rode her as hard as I could towards the end of the valley, after this conversation, to try and let some of the steam out of my ears. I was gone two days. By the time I got back, grimy and sunburned, John Fennick was dead. Killed by a wall that knifed him in the back. Some people tried to say I was somehow responsible, but the circumstances of the murder were so coincidental, most of the town realized I would have had to have been a magician to have executed such a deed.

All along the outside walls of the gardens were stone seats where you could stop and sit if you were weary. They were low to the ground, in keeping with the other artifacts of the town, but useful for drunks and those carrying loads under a midday sun. Some of the old men had chosen favourite positions on busy pedestrian routes and would occupy these seats from dawn till dusk. Their lives already having gone by, they liked to watch others flow past. John Fennick had apparently been imbibing at an inn during the evening of his death and staggered home with a companion just after midnight.

The upper part of the town is built into the hillside on the edge of the valley, and while the Fennick place commanded a drop-away view of the paved streets down to the river, and the terraced slopes on the far side, it was a cruel climb. The drystone walls, with their occasional cool slate seats, were indeed well-suited to prevent punishment to limb and lung. John Fennick had sat on one of these while his friend, less able, had leaned one-handed against the wall further down, to gather his breath. Suddenly, according to his drunken companion, Fennick gave out an almighty scream, thrashed around for a few seconds, then slumped forward, "his arms dangling like an ape's, to his ankles."

People came out of their houses at that point, while racing adrenalin sobered the other fellow more rapidly than any synthetic drug. They found Fennick's body had been pierced through by a sword-long blade sprung from a crack in the wall behind the seats. The point of the instrument protruded a good twelve inches from his chest. The scene further dramatized. On arrival in the valley the occupants of the house had planted wisteria to cover the bare wall. Plants grow very rapidly in the valley, given the right treatment, and the wisteria had covered the wall. John Fennick had clutched at the plant in his death throes and pulled it across his body like a purple cloak.

By the time I arrived back in town, they had dismantled the mechanism in the wall and it afforded a great deal of mystery. As an instrument of murder it was elaborately fashioned. That the assassin was among ourselves was soon dismissed (much to my own relief), and the blame was placed on the town's former occupants. The length of the blade and considerable force behind the spring suggested that it was designed to penetrate a thick, squat anatomy.

The operation of the mechanism was fairly complex. It entailed simultaneous pressure on three points, two of them being supplied by a second party: in this case Fennick's companion, who had pressed just the right brick in the wall, while his left foot rested on a paving stone — the second trigger. The third was a depression which must have been activated by Fennick's elbow, near to the point in the brickwork where the lethal blade existed. So complex were the mechanical functions of the instrument, with its intricate levers and pulleys and cogs, and so complicated the operation, it seemed almost a ritual killing. Certainly as a murder weapon it was too elaborate, and why rely on your victim to supply essential assistance in his own killing? If it was necessary to have such a machine, why not just a single lever?

At least these unanswered questions absolved me from suspicion of being implicated. The very detail of the clockwork killer must have taken lengthy planning and infinite care in construction on the part of a skilled craftsman: quite apart from the fact that I would have had to strip down the wall and pavement before the eyes of the other citizens. In any case it brought Sally no closer to my side. She spent her time consoling the distraught friend of John Fennick, whom she married a short while afterwards.

"She didn't deserve a runt like you anyhow," snorted Thel on the day of the wedding as I mooned around feeling sorry for myself. Baker grunted his own approval of these sentiments, at the same time burning out his nostrils with grade-nine snuff.

Some time later I took a job with Jenny Ledbetter's father on his orange plantation to the south of the town. While he didn't encourage my advances towards Jenny, he didn't warn me off either; and since Jenny and I worked side-by-side in the fields, it was difficult to keep us apart. A feeling sort of *grew* between us, rather than flash-fired into sudden existence, and soon we were exchanging confidences. I found she had a lively mind. Thel was right — I did find it a necessary element in our relationship. In fact, and I don't mind admitting it, Jenny was cleverer than me in many ways. Perhaps not as shrewd, but her knowledge was wider-based and more informed than my own. I was stronger, physically. (This may seem a superfluous statement, but Thel was a woman and she could have broken me in two anytime she felt like it.) We fell in love, gradually. The bond was stronger for it.

The town had a very strange effect on us all. It was a negative influence, and some put it down to godliness, or luck, or something mystical in our culture. But most of us realized it was the town. The fact was, after a year, no one had fallen ill. Normally, in a population the size of ours there was always

someone down with a complaint. On average we should have had
two dozen sick at any one time. But the truth was, after those
people who had fallen ill during the journey had become well —
or died — there was no more disease. No more insanity, even. The
old people died occasionally, of physical complaints — heart
failure mostly — but even they tended towards a fitness unknown
before. Those that had suffered from things like arthritis still had
their problems but to a much lesser degree. The doctors
complained that they felt defunct. Broken bones mended rapidly
and without complications. Only one premature death marred
that year: John Fennick's. A woman who fell from a hay loft and
fractured her skull and was expected to die, recovered in a
miraculously short period of time. Further out in the valley one
could sense a change in the air. Perhaps there was a central point,
a key building, like the church, which affected all within a limited
sphere of influence.

With the beautiful growing conditions, the balmy weather and
the lack of physical and mental illness, it was near enough to
heaven. The bible says three score years and ten, and it seemed we
were going to get our due whether we liked it or not. Aside from
mechanical assassins of course, but you can't tear apart a granite-
built town of alien interlocking blocks, engineered to withstand
millenniums, with the handtools of colonists.

(Now that I can look back I think I can see some of the logic
behind the alien devices. The elderly, in fact, live well past their
biblical quota, and do so in fitness and health. Many of our
earlier deaths — and the lingering physical handicaps like
arthritis — were overlaps from our former life. Now we are
perfect, and when we die, *when*, we go out *phut* like a candle. No
cancers dragging our bodies slowly over talons of pain. No
bloated limbs or malignant, creeping sores. No terrible inner
dark passages to navigate alone.)

But paradise has its own drawbacks. It can be excrutiatingly
boring. Thel and Baker hated it. So did I, to a lesser degree.

I was with Thel and Baker when the explosion thundered
through the streets of the town. We stared into each other's eyes in
fright and incomprehension. On recovering, I was the first out of
the door, followed by Thel, then Baker. The floating debris of our
church tower was still disturbing the otherwise peaceful evening.

The great pear-shaped bell, inherited from our unseen aliens, had exploded.

We surveyed the mess: half our adopted church had been destroyed. Two bodies had already been carried out and a third was beneath the collapsed masonry.

"What the hell was that for?" growled Thel, angrily.

Baker shrugged and I murmured something about, "Crazy natives."

We began levering stonework and timber from the top of the pile, but there was little hope of finding a survivor underneath. Each of us had that little question "Why?" buzzing around in our brains the whole time we worked. Thel kept insisting that we had done the aliens no harm — a fact we were all fully aware of — so why should they leave booby traps all over the place?

"It's only one," I said.

"Two," she reminded me. "There was also Fennick."

"*Yeah*, Fennick," emphasized Baker.

They were right of course. There could have been dozens of similar devices scattered throughout the town. We worked on into the night under lights, but the third person was dead. After we found him we slowed down. There was no real rush to complete the job.

It seemed most of the town came out to finish the clearance, and whereas the majority of us had fallen into a lethargic, apathetic way of life, the fires were burning again. There were offers from carpenters and masons to rebuild the church, bigger and better than before. A glazier spoke of stained glass, something that had not been part of the original building. And a real bell-shaped bell was proposed by a guild of metalworkers. Tilers wanted to replace the old flooring with mosaic. Someone proposed widening the doorway and fitting solid wood doors. There was a great deal of enthusiasm.

Of course, it was a tragedy and there was a pall of sorrow on the shoulders of a few. Grief is private amongst us though, and we left the mourners to their tears. Someone, Baker I think, suggested we take some men and search outside the valley for the culprits, but the idea was not taken seriously. We were all too busy planning. There was a feverish kind of excitement in the air that was difficult to quell, even on the day of the funeral.

The aftermath included an inquiry into the cause of the explosion — the trigger, that is. After a great deal of deliberation the experts told us that it was pure chance that had caused the bomb to explode. The explanation was barely credible.

The great bell had had a clapper inside, but there was not a man or woman in the town strong enough to swing the beast to get it to sound. Since we liked the two ends of the day to be chimed in and out, the priests had been a little upset by the immovable metal pear dangling leaden from its enormous joist. The problem had been solved by gathering a pile of large pebbles from the bank of the river. Youths were engaged to hurl the missiles at the bell at prescribed hours of the day. One of these stones had detonated the bomb.

That a rock should accurately strike the inch-square detonator to the booby trap was not, in itself, unusual. In the course of time one of the boys would be bound to hit it: one year, a hundred years, they stood as much chance of hitting that spot as any other. But — the bell was not designed for stone throwers. It had a clapper and the clapper would not have activated the charge in an eternity. Its striking circle was two feet away from the detonator. Also, the bomb needed a second pressure point within the church. Someone had to be standing on a particular slab in the room we used as a vestry. In this case, it had been a priest, who was unharmed by the explosion.

The chances of *accidentally* detonating the so-called "booby trap" were incredibly low.

"So what the hell did they do it for?" said Baker. "We could have been here a million years and not set it off."

"It's not only the bomb," I said to them. "What about John Fennick's death? I think that was a *kind* of accident too."

"Well, what is it then?" cried Thel, throwing her hands into the air. We all stared at one another without understanding. At that time I had just the smokiest notion of what lay behind the murders; clarification came later, after several more incidents, but by that time Thel and Baker had gone.

For two years no other freak booby traps entered our lives. We prospered. The vineyards and citrus fruit groves yielded their plenty; our livestock multiplied; from the river we reaped harvests of migrating fish. The community was in a comfortable position — no one wanted for food, clothing or shelter. Our only complaint might have been the dull routine. Life turned over, regularly, like the wheel of a clock: click, click, click, click.

"I'm going," said Thel one day, and she took a pack horse and went. Just like that. Something had snapped inside her. Baker had already gone with a contingent of young men and women. A break-away colonist group that wanted to push further into the interior. No doubt Thel intended catching them up, but she didn't say so. She waved until she was out of sight. I missed her terribly.

I stayed because I was married to Jenny and had responsibilities about the farm. Jenny was my anchor but, damn, I stretched the chain really tight the day Thel left. It almost snapped.

In the fifth year we had one or two minor incidents connected with the aliens. A cavity wall let out some noxious gas which killed a dog. A hearthstone suddenly spat a coloured dart into a family group who were having their evening meal. It stuck in the wooden handle of the stew bowl, right in line with one of the children. A door released a blade which severed two fingers from a woman's hand. These incidents caused a flurry of excitement amongst the community for some while after each occurrence.

Seven years after came a very dramatic death. A politician in the middle of a campaign speech threw his arms into the air and plunged thirty feet down Speaker's Steps. There was an arrow of a strange design protruding from his chest. It was believed to have been fired from a drainpipe on the side of our town hall. Putting the death aside, one could admire the intricate workmanship of the arrow, especially its flexible, folding, lacework flights. It was a beautiful, if deadly piece of craft.

I think by that time we had guessed the intentions of the aliens, who had built the town for themselves, after all, and not for us. Some of our people were for abandoning the place, and indeed one or two did leave in search of Baker's group, but the majority accepted a change in philosophy. We *allowed* a fragment of alien culture to enter our own, to fuse with it and become part of our way of life. Indeed, we *had* to accept it, or follow Baker. After living for so long in the valley, we had become attuned to its faults — its *one* flaw in it was that there was no flaw.

That this paradox should affect us as it obviously did the aliens, only showed how close we were to them in certain aspects. We had common ground in a loathing of unalterable rhythm. The natural (and supernatural) influences of the valley ordered our lives into harmony too constant to be acceptable. We needed the occasional hiccough to alter the pace, the timing, of our existence. *Heaven should not be without risk.*

The aliens had realized themselves that a life without change produces inertia. No new songs, no new poetry, no artistic progress. A Spartan existence eventually dies from apathy. So they built tragedy into their lives by patterning secret places of their town with deadly toys. Like toymakers, they had delighted in the design and mechanics of their devices: subtle, ingenious machineries as well as grand, dramatic objects pregnant with thunder.

Sorrow, yes, but excitement too. A flicker in the lifeline. A talking point.

"Did you hear ...?"

Without them, the unalterable days follow each other like blank cards. All sense of time is lost and the brain blunts its edge. With them, celebrities are created; the reluctant widow, the heroic father. There is no need for blood feuds or vendettas. Our lives are tricked into alertness. Not only do we have the incidents themselves to snap us into enthusiasm for life, we have the presence of all the still-hidden devices to consider. Every man, every woman is at constant risk, albeit that risk may be small.

We, each of us, have to look over our shoulder, keep our mental faculties primed, our reactions swift, for we are all potential targets. Lethargy will not be our inheritance.

And where did the aliens go? Some believe they moved on, for whatever reasons they may have had. I personally think they will return, which is not such a bad thing. There's room for both of us in the valley, and the interest we will create in each other will add further zest to our separate cultures. Perhaps they migrate to the mountains or the sea — to return x number of years later, a different generation — one that has no blueprints, no knowledge of the position of the devices?

Which pocket of rock in the town bears my name? I sit and wonder. Could I live without Jenny, or she without me? Will our

son grow to manhood? A personal tragedy may have me hating
the aliens and their tricky innovations — but the community as a
whole will be rewarded with vivid images of death. My widow will
be a queen in black. I will visit her grave in the orange grove, to
place flowers and words upon the grass. My parentless son will
have a trace of iron in his expression. Suffering creates
character.

We could all grow old and die in our beds — but there is a
chance, just a chance, that one of us will die young and beautiful.
Such things are written in songs. To be remembered is
immortality.

GOD'S COLD LIPS

The eyelids hung, heavy as shields, and opened with great difficulty to reveal a polished sky. The bright yellow shape twisted and warped, floating like an amoeba before him, splitting into smaller cells that danced apart, then plunged together again. Finally he managed to focus and turned his face away from the sun with annoyance, a small growl escaping his throat.

The sound worried him but he was feeling too drowsy to follow the thought to a conclusion. He knew that he was not unwell but merely recovering from a long sleep. He lifted his arm slowly and with great effort to his mouth — and tasted fur. *The transmutation had been a success.* Rolling on to his side he began falling into a deep sleep again.

"Switch off the overhead lights," he heard a voice saying softly. "Let him rest. Tomorrow his system will have absorbed. . . ." The rest was lost in the humming of his brain. He fell asleep again with the strong smell of sweetstick burning his olfactory lobes.

He was Adam Marillac — or was he? He certainly wasn't the tiger — that was merely the fur, flesh and bone that housed his soul. He felt nothing like a large cat; he felt like Marillac, swallowed. In fact, he thought, he was neither of these animals. He was an idea, an abstract enthusiasm in another man's mind. An experiment.

"How are you feeling? You look . . . well, like a tiger." The hands came up in a defensive gesture. Steen added, "I trust you are comfortable? There's a silver stud in your ear — an identification disc of sorts. You'll need it later when we come to take you home."

He dipped his eyelids. It still hurt to move quickly.

Steen continued. "We'll let you out into the jungle in a few days — I trust you're ready for it? No worries?"

No worries? Of course he was worried. More than that, he was terrified. The jungle was a thick web of black and green, of damp horror. A tiger may be unconcerned by spiders, indifferent to snakes. Adam Marillac was terrorstruck at the sight of either creature. The thought of them made his throat muscles constrict involuntarily with fear. The jungle was full of snakes and spiders. The jungle was full of all those nightmares which had haunted him through childhood and into maturity.

Childhood had been spent in the usual way: kindergarten, school, university. Marillac tried to remember a single event of his childhood that was not related to one of these institutions — and failed. They took in an infant at four years old and from that point onwards, until the time came to find a job, they smothered the child with learning, administered within the surrounds of plastimetal furnishings and endless banyan buildings. Marillac had only once before stood under the unscreened harshness of a starlit, summer sky. Had only once throughout manhood sat on dangerously-damp meadowgrass in the wild atmosphere of a light breeze. Had, that single time, smelled the hostile fumes of wild flowers. The excursion outside the city had been necessary to complete his education and he, like all the others, had been frightened by the weird sounds and the vast openness of the outside world.

But he had promised to live in the environment for which his new body was suited — at least for a time. Six months or so they said — barring accidents. Barring complications. Barring death from inside the tiger, or from without.

It was difficult adjusting to his new role, albeit temporary, in life. As yet his body was unco-ordinated and he tended to make foolish mistakes with the heavy limbs. Steen said he would get used to them quite quickly.

But then Steen was no expert on gaining control of an animal's body, a big cat's body: there were no experts. Steen was merely the sponsor for his transmutation. Together they were supposed to be striving to put together a paper — but it was Marillac who was taking all the risks. Steen just sat back and watched, pulling away affectedly on that old-fashioned drug of his.

When Marillac had first realized he was going to become a tiger he had studied them, both from books and in captivity. One thing had endeared them to him, a single trait — they were solitary beasts. Marillac was a loner and always had been. He had been married once but was now divorced. It was the marital state, the togetherness, that had been wrong, not his choice of bride. She had never understood why he left so suddenly.

Now he was really alone, divorced from the human race by a barrier only skin-thick, but impenetrable. Soon he would be entering that terrible jungle, undefended by the technology of Man. It was a sobering thought that he would have to kill, at close quarters, with his bare ... claws? ... to live.

They were standing inside the giant gates, before which lay the jungles. Nothing stood between himself and Steen, but the man held a stun rod as self-consciously as a new general holds his rank, and other pale, brittle men stood nearby, arms folded to make sharp triangles. Already Marillac felt alienated, untrustworthy. What did they expect he might do — swing a pawful of dagger-like claws suddenly at Steen's head? This was all uncalled for, somewhat farcical. He even liked Steen a little.

"Well, old chap," said Steen, swinging the stun rod by his side like a baton. "Hope you don't get too bored. We'll put some cooked meat by the gate each day for a while — you won't feel up to hunting for a bit." He paused and pulled on his sweetstick, then added, "It is important, you know. A lot of people will thank you for it later."

Or not, thought Marillac. They wouldn't thank him if the thing was a failure — even if it was just the idea that failed. The breeze was changing direction and he lifted his nose to it. No longer did the sweat of those armpits, or the fumes from Steen's stick, hang heavy in his nostrils. Now the scents of the jungle came to him: heady smells of fringe grasses, indefinable scents of strange animals, and underlying all else the deep odour of damp leaves. He felt a sense of anticipation mingling with his fear.

The following day the same sunlight that poured gold on to the grasslands at the jungle's edge ran fingers of fire down his flanks, playing on the black transverse stripes of his hide like a harpist. Was that psychological? Because he knew that black absorbed the light while the red-gold between the bars reflected it? Possibly, but he liked the sensation, even if it was mental rather than physical. He was beginning to become attuned to the new body — beginning to accept it for what it was. Marillac could never have imagined the pleasures of a cat before he had experienced them. They were more than sensual, they were sexual. The touch of the warm wind on the white belly-fur. The smell of musk thickening the air.

Being closer to the ground was an experience in itself. The hardbaked earth had its own beautiful smells, warm zones and traces of small creatures.

The jungle's border loomed before him, its black and impenetrable ribcage dripping with green and heaving like the flanks of some giant beast in the pulsing midday sun. He would not enjoy entering this living jungle. His jungle had been the steel corridors and compartments of his world, the dangers of which walked on two legs and in packs.

He stayed on the fringe of the undergrowth that night, starting every few minutes or so at the sounds of the lower orders of .wildlife in the grass. (While the human in him was afraid of the jungle's darkness and its unknown terrors, what was left of the tiger disliked being out in the open and vulnerable under a moonlit sky.)

When the morning came he tried to rationalize the two warring instincts inside him, and decided that the *tiger* had the less sensible of the two arguments, for a tiger's only enemy is Man — and Marillac at least had nothing to fear from that quarter. Nevertheless he had to enter the jungle sometime and it was better to do it in the light of day, fortified by a full stomach. Marillac pulled himself to his feet and padded towards the gate, and food.

They had lied to him.

Of course, now that he was thinking more clearly, now that the drugs had left his body, he could see that it would have been foolish to give him cooked meat. If he became reliant upon the handouts of food prepared for human consumption he might never leave the vicinity of the gate and hunt for himself. Hence he would not pass into that ribcage of trees except perhaps for water. That would not be "living the life of a tiger in its own environment".

Moreover, the raw meat was still in the shape it had employed as a living thing: it was some kind of antelope; horns, hoofs and warm skin. Warm? Marillac sniffed at the nostrils of the creature.

It had not long been killed — perhaps a few minutes earlier.
There was a neat hole burnt through its heart. He couldn't eat
that, not a beautiful creature still retaining the ember-warmth of
life. The whole idea was repugnant to him.

As he trotted towards the trees without having tasted the food
he realized that after two or three days there would probably be
no meat of any kind by the gate. They would force him away from
his last touch with civilization, using his hunger as a spur. That
Steen character, that smooth-talking bastard Steen, had
manoeuvred Marillac into this ugly position. Clammy nightmares threatened him from outside, and he, Marillac — timid
little clown, cosseted throughout his childhood because of ill
health — was trapped within. There was no choice now. He
began to panic and could feel that cat-heart pumping quickly
beneath the fur. He was really trapped. He could throw his heavy-
boned body at the gates and roar for all he was worth . . . no one
would come, because they *knew* he had to eat, and to eat he had to
find prey. He had to kill. They had him . . . Steen had him, just
where he wanted him.

Marillac stopped at the edge of the trees and realized he was
growling loudly. He pulled his mind back to his present situation
with a jerk. It was tigerish, not human, to growl at the thought of
revenge.

Close to, the trees were not as formidable as they had
previously appeared, and with a preliminary cat-like sniff of the
stifling air before him he entered. It *was* dark inside, but more of a
comforting darkness than a frightening one, and he could smell
water nearby. He would drink the water and then he would sleep.
It was a very thick, humid heat that enveloped his fur, damping it.
He suddenly realized how tired he felt — the hot day, not the
night, was the time to fall asleep.

The leaves brushed against his glossy coat and he felt his
powerful muscles gliding easily under the skin. He was power
itself. Only the elephant could outmatch him for strength, and
that was a huge, clumsy beast, unworthy of even standing
together with the tiger. Marillac was grace, was speed, was
fierceness, was lashing, spitting, frightening power. Before he
reached the pool he could hear the other animals scuttling away
through the undergrowth. *They* were afraid of *him*. He growled

with pleasure. No one had ever been afraid of Marillac before.

In the half-light he drank the brackish water, taking in weed and dead floating insects. As he drank he heard a noise above him. At first it was the sound of lizards running over waxy leaves, but it swiftly built up volume until it was a thundering roar that made him begin growling again, until the drops eventually soaked through the thick foliage further to wet his fur and he realized what it was: a tropical rainstorm.

The rain only lasted an hour, but during that time it was as intense as any waterfall. And afterwards the steam created such a heavy atmosphere that he fell into the sleep he desired, which lasted until nightfall.

That night he went back to the gate and ate the soft organs in the underside of the antelope, tearing open the gut and thrusting his face inside amongst the rank-smelling entrails. He hoped that Steen could not hear him. He felt he was debasing what was left of Marillac, but the hunger had to be satisfied. To his surprise he did not vomit, and afterwards, with the gore still hanging from his spreading facial hairs, he made his way back to the jungle to clean himself, determined to put distance between himself and the gate through which he was sure Steen was spying on him.

Marillac had met Steen for the first time at the university where they had both been lecturers — Marillac in the cartography of near space and Steen in zoology. Both had an interest in the idea of adaptation to planetary or even local outside environments by exchanging the shell that housed the "mortal coil". Transmutation experiments, animal to animal, had been carried out with a great deal of success but they had that element of the unknown which made men recoil from any suggestion that humans might benefit from such a rearrangement. People who had been moulded by their environment of enclosed cities were now the victims of their own protective measures. By isolating themselves from the elements they had made themselves dependent upon their own overcrowded but safe enclosures. They were weak, sickly, wan creatures for whom transmutation was a Godsend — if any of them dared to try it. People were not adverse to changing bodies to save their lives but they were afraid of losing "themselves" as they were. They were afraid of "dying" within another body.

Once it had been confirmed that Marillac was wasting away because of an unknown disease which would relegate his body to a hoverchair, he resigned himself to the fact that he would have to change bodies, ready or not. He had to pay for the treatment, however, by offering six months of his life to Steen's experiments. Steen, being a zoologist, was naturally fascinated by the idea of getting "inside" an animal to learn of its ways, habits and fears. That he was too afraid to follow the desire through himself was plainly obvious, but what choice did Marillac have? Having no control over one's muscles meant an unpleasant life in which uncleanliness took over as a matter of course. The thought alone was repulsive to him.

The tiger came to a river that threw itself, like something hell-bent on destruction, down the glades and over molar rocks. Never before had Marillac seen anything so beautiful, and it made him forget his hunger for a time. Green plants dipped spidery legs gingerly into pools, and others, like scalps, hung loosely over the waterfall washing their strands. A tall white bird fished with its sword-like beak in the waters below, treading warily amongst the rocks. It stabbed once, twice, and came out with a frog which disappeared in a flash down the sapling throat. Marillac desperately needed food — he had had nothing for two days. Settling down below the waterfall he allowed its thunder to lull him into a dream-like state while he kept his eyes open for signs of life. Some time afterwards a frog leapt on to the bank and stared at the immobile tiger. He flattened it with a quick paw and gulped it down. Several more went the same way. Even a small, once-feared snake met this unhappy fate.

Shortly after he had eaten, the moon appeared over the trees and poured its cold light upon the jungle floor. There were men up there on that satellite, looking for useful minerals, building underground cities. Once he was back in the body of a man Marillac hoped to join them — and those on Mars. In his mind he began to recite the names of the pioneers of Mars: Lecker, Spitzendon, Alvaraz . . . but after three he stopped, unable to remember the fourth or subsequent explorers. He had always known them before — as a child he could reel off the first thirteen names without even thinking. Lecker, Spitzendon, Alvarez ... Alvarez ... but what did it matter? He had far more important things to consider than the colonization of the plants. (He *meant* "planets". Why did he think "plants"?) Colonization. Governments had vague ideas about colonizing the outer planets, but were concerned with Man's physical ability to cope with the extreme conditions.

What if men were to change their bodies for those of animals? rumbled a theorist. Animals that could withstand extreme temperatures, varying pressures? No one bothered to mention the other drawbacks — the lack of oxygenated atmosphere in which to work, the lack of food sources, the several other necessities of life which were not present on the planets. Why should they? It was another avenue of pure research, dear to people like Steen, that could be played with for several years before someone with common sense in a responsible position realized that money was being wasted.

A beetle crawled from beneath a leaf at his feet. He stared at it, curious to see what its mission was. The antennae waved and danced from its brow and its armoured legs picked cautiously at the ground beneath them. Were there beetles on other planets? he wondered. He did not care for creatures like this, but all the same he was allowing it to pass over his paw for some distance before flicking it off. Perhaps the moon was crawling with beetles? No, that was idiotic — there was no life native to the moon. Then why did he see these black, slow-limbed creatures picking their way across lunar webs — and why the visions of holes in the ground crawling with life? Men? They must be men, he thought. Spidermen on the moon. But even that seemed foolish and soon he dismissed the images from his mind.

That night, with his strength partially returned, he swam the swift river and on the far bank had his first successful hunt. Breaking cover by the water's edge he had come across a herd of wild pigs, and with his scent hidden in the billowing spray of the waterfall had brought down one of their young. He was surprised at how easy it was. Marillac had held the kicking creature down with his weight and had sunk his teeth into the beast's bloated

belly. It screamed shrilly close to his ear and he almost let it go in
surprise, but after a while the noise stopped and he could feel
warm blood running along his lip. Ravenous, he tore open the
skin and fed on the meat. In the moonlight the animal's eyes
glazed as death came up fast and finally overtook it.

The day was always hot. He blamed it for his fuzzy thinking and
for the way his feverish mind ran amok with unreal scenes.
Perhaps he did have a fever? Animals became sick the same as
humans. He was crossing the grassy plains, between the jungles,
and game was abundant. But the sun was merciless as he
searched for some shade under which to rest. His head pounded
and every vestige of contentment left him when he could find no
cool place under which to lie. A thorn bush or even a single tree.
He knew he was a Mongolian and was only just shedding the last
of his thick winter coat. Steen had not worried too much about
species.

"Just a tiger," he had said, when Marillac had had the temerity
to broach the subject, "nothing special about it. A big one, of
course. Can't have you getting into a fight and coming out the
loser can we?"

Just a tiger, three feet tall at the shoulder and packed solid with
muscle. A giant beast reaching fourteen feet in length. Just a
tiger?

"Is a tiger very strong?" Marillac had asked.

"Strong? My God, there are some stories about tigers you just
wouldn't believe. He's one of the most powerful of the land
mammals."

With these words Steen must have known he would strike
home. A man as weak as a kitten, whose own muscles refused to
answer the simplest of demands, would of course be impressed by
strength.

"Even the pachyderms are afraid of tigers," said Steen.
"They . . ."

The stories, old wives' tales stirred into a modicum of truth, fell
on eager ears. Who would not want to be a lord for six months of
his life, afraid of nothing, omnipotent among the beasts of the
field? Certainly not a wasted man in Marillac's condition. . . .

In the clearing were some stone ruins, covered in vines without and ulcerated by fungi within. There were some walls, almost hidden beneath grass and moss, and in the centre of the disturbed, roughly-hewn stones was an old temple, the eaves curling at the edges like dying leaves. Spiders' webs spanned the points of these eaves like the frail hands of ghosts.

The tiger made its way up steps littered with chips of quartz and twigs, and paused at the tall entrance. Inside it was black and smelled of a dynasty that patronized the night and gave gifts of men's lives to a dark god. Entering, the first stone altar was blood-black where once long knives sang and struck; the second supported a cross-legged, green stone idol the height of three men. The god had lightning cracks running through its torso, and the upper limbs, outstretched to receive its blood-drenched offerings, were stained and spotted with bird lime.

The three eyes were cold, hard and unreadable. They followed the tiger as it moved slowly around its base. Scratched on the block underneath, probably by some theologically ignorant subaltern of a foreign army, he read the words: *Brahma, Vishnu or Siva?* Under this misconception it said, *5th Infantry Brigade, the jungle bums.* Then simply, *Harris.* No rank? thought Marillac. The writer must have been a conscript. All regulars were proud of their rank, whether private or general.

Marillac stared again at the face of the stone idol. The eyes regarded him steadily and made the fur rise on his back. The figure exuded a heavy air of malevolence, a wickedness that time had only succeeded in bringing to the surface of its shiny features. Its gaze was steeped in the knowledge of victimized children, struggling during the last throes of life. The high-cheekboned smile had grinned through a thousand attempts to sate its lust for the limbs of young women. And the glittering third eye, serving as navel in the overhanging belly, stared at its own gross parts.

Marillac's body was chilled to the heart. This was no god he knew of, no known religion. It filled him with dread. It was the god of some small dark age where men had lost themselves. An age during which they stood rigid with fear at the sound of the temple gongs, and prayed that their god might go blind, or that some new benign presence would shatter it to fragments and take its place.

He left the halls quickly despite his fatigue, vowing never to return. Outside he found a new, very real, danger awaiting his exit from the temple's black interior. At the foot of the steps, head cocked to one side in a typical feline pose, was another tiger.

Marillac paused and steadied himself. This was something he had not bargained for. This was the materialization of another of Steen's lies. Marillac was supposed to be the only tiger in the vicinity.

Now what did he do? The other half-shadow beast had risen to its feet and was regarding him steadfastly. It was definitely smaller than he was — a different variety. Its coat was a deep orange and black, in contrast to the pale, fuzzy markings that cut across Marillac. He could, he decided quickly, outrun this smaller beast if it became necessary. Perhaps, he thought wildly, the new tiger was another experiment? Another trapped man like himself — unable to tell him of his condition?

The tiger had covered three steps upward before Marillac growled involuntarily. The other stopped, seemingly puzzled. Would it know instinctively that he was a human in disguise? Would it smell his fear and know him for a man? *Would he have to kill this other animal in order to save himself?* My God, thought Marillac, there's only one person I could kill right now, and that's Steen.

The smaller tiger began climbing again, cautiously. Marillac drew back his lips into a snarl and then gave out a hostile roar. Still it came, until the man-tiger could smell the sweet odours to which his body, if not his mind, knew how to respond. There was to be no battle. Possibly a union, but no fight.

Some months later the two tigers reached the foot of the mountains and climbed up into the cooler air. The female was pregnant and the larger male, with the silver stud in his ear, wished to leave her in a place safe for the cubs before making a journey which he knew was inevitable.

They had had a good summer together, hunting and eating well; she had taught him the art of such a livelihood. A small Sumatran, wearing her black-orange colours loudly, she would drive the game to him and he would make the kill. Once he had adjusted to a certain state of mind their teamwork became unbeatable, despite their mismatched camouflage. In the last jungle, set aside to cater for all the homeless animal species from all five continents, the wildlife was abundant.

His body suffered, at times, from sores and chronic bladder complaints. Towards the latter she was silently sympathetic. But his sores were something she could actively doctor, by licking them clean for him where he could not reach himself, her spittle helping to disinfect the wounds.

It was a simple life and in the early weeks he had thought he would go mad with boredom, but as time passed he found that hunting, resting, eating and caring for the other partner was a full existence with little time left for brooding. He found more and more that he had to think like a tiger to survive. She became angry when he made mistakes and chastized him with a sharpness that overrode his greater strength. He did not like that, and pleasing her became his prime incentive in life. He slipped into an unreal state of mind. Unreal, that is, to Marillac's old way of thinking.

The mountains were not the place to spend the winter, but they were remote and the need for protection was strong in both the tigers. He settled her in a spot where small game and tall grass were plentiful, and eagles were scarce. There he left her.

The compulsion to retrace his wanderings was strong and there was a peculiar buzzing in his brain which he guessed was to do with the silver stud in his ear. She had tried to tear the thing out with her teeth but the pain had been too much and eventually he had pushed her away with a swing of his paw. It still hung on to the torn flesh of his ear. His mind and this thing were moving his legs, running them in the direction of the place whence he had come. His heavy bulk trod lightly through the jungle on the springs that were his muscles and the pads that were his feet. A face kept showing itself to his mind. There were other associated pictures which accompanied the face. He was vaguely aware that the man who owned that face had a name, but the buzzing in his mind would not allow him to stop and consider what that name was. He pushed on, into the depths of the trees, towards the shouting river.

(". . . Remember Marillac, if you become lost we can find you with the scanners. That stud in your ear not only identifies you to us, but also transmits a signal . . . We shall be waiting for you at the time of the autumn equinox — by the gate. . . . If not we'll search for you, so you won't be imprisoned within that body forever. Just play the tiger . . . we depend on you. . . .")

He swam the river, narrower than before since no rain had fallen for some time and the spring snows had all gone from the mountains. Coming out on the far side he rested on the bank, drying his wet, plastered coat until it fluffed shaggy again in warm breezes. He dreamed cat dreams of waterholes in the sun; of his female tiger turning in mock anger as he tried to mount her at the wrong time; of the electric ecstasy when it was the right time and the warmth of her coat burned into his breast; of the buck brought down in full flight amid choking dust; of the horned mother driving towards his belly as he strove to make off with his kill. These were the dreams of a cat and there were none better.

The buzzing sounded again. He had forgotten it on hitting the cool water. It must have ceased its noise while he was swimming. Now it was like a hornet loose inside his skull, tormenting him. Destroying his dreams. He lifted himself to his feet, the left hind leg giving him trouble where he had bruised it under the weight of that buck. He felt clean and fresh and strong, though. His tendons pulled at thick limbs that had never bent in servitude. His shoulders heaved at the front of a broad back that would carry no burden. He was the tiger, feared by all. Even the snakes and spiders which he had once loathed were to him a matter of indifference.

(". . . We want to know, at the end of it all, whether you have managed to adjust to your environment — whether you fit the role for which your body was designed. Above all, we want to know if, psychologically, you . . . well, frankly, if you're still sane . . . The stresses of such an experiment. . . .")

He began his journey again. There was not much further to go. The edge of the jungle was only one day's walk.

(". . . You *will* be in your right mind, of course. You're the ideal candidate for such . . . I mean you've been imprisoned in a useless body for some time now. It'll be a release for you, to be able to walk, run and roam at will — like a return to childhood. . . .")

* * *

He broke out into the clearing at a run. It was past noon and the sun was behind him. Their scent had been strong for some time, rank in his nostrils: it quickened his heartbeat and he felt himself afraid. All his instincts rebelled against this meeting. They were men, and he had been — was still — a tiger. He could see them waiting for him by the gate, their hands shielding their eyes. As he neared them he slowed to a trot, searching the faces. They had weapons. But the faces? One, no. Two, no. Three ... yes! The name finally flashed into his mind: *Steen*? He *had* remembered at the last moment.

Steen was smiling. Constructed thoughts struggled to the surface of the tiger's mind. The man was smiling because the experiment had been a success. They had done it together, the pair of them: two human minds and a tiger's body.

He slowed to an uneasy walk in front of them, and they all began talking at once, laughing, gesturing and pointing at the silver stud in his ear. The movements were too quick, the sounds alien, and he hesitated, stepping backwards. The weapons of the men were lowered from their obvious positions, the owners seemingly embarrassed by their weight. They hung them down by their legs, almost out of sight behind their billowing clothes. And Steen was smiling, sweetstick in his teeth, nodding to his colleagues, each nod saying, "I told you we'd make it — only the debriefing to go — matter of formality ... Look at my tiger: sleek coat, muscled frame, bright eyes, strong jaws, and sane as Sunday. ..."

The scent of the sweetstick wafted around Steen's head and was funnelled to the tiger by the wheeling breezes. It clogged his sensitive organs and red mist began clouding his confused brain. The already-present adrenalin, making the blood surge through his veins, increased, until the fear drummed panic in his ears and his nerves were taut with terror. Someone coughed sharply and Steen's hand jerked out, too fast. The net spread, a flimsy bird-wing shape, above the tiger's head. The guns came up and hooks appeared in ready hands. It was clumsy. The net floated out and fell short. The gangling creatures were unskilled at capturing live beasts.

"Get him," yelled Steen. An engine whined to life and a mechanical open-mouthed cage swept through the gates and descended upon the tiger.

The startled beast sprang from three yards away, jaws snapping at the narrow face. An object went spinning through the air like a smoking twig. Steen went down, his spine snapping under the full weight of a mature tiger, his scream quenched. The shock had killed him before the big cat tossed his body aside like a pet's toy.

Before the other men had recovered from the sudden attack the tiger was halfway back towards the jungle's edge. Then came the sound of thunder and the noise of hummingbirds caught in the tall dry grass. Just prior to entering the green darkness a stinging pain made him snap at his hindquarters. Then coolness closed over him, brushing his body as he made his way through it with rapid movements. The pain in his rear continued, but it was bearable. Not a death wound, merely a heavy discomfort. He rested, breathing hard, the blood still racing.

Men would pursue him now. Hunt him down like a maneater of old. They would come as noisy birds, and stoop like eagles out of the sun. They would come trundling like warthogs with their hands full of death — and they had their own ways to follow his spoor, to track him by his scent. The buzzing in his ear had already started again.

The first of the pursuers came into the jungle cautiously and he hid, lying on his belly in the thick undergrowth. They passed on either side of him, having nothing with them with which to see through the leaves. He was tempted to attack when the offensive odour was all around and his sinews were tight with apprehension. When their smells had drifted away he began tearing at his ear with sharp claws, pulling, pulling, trying to scratch out the silver leech which drove him mad by singing like a field full of crickets. Later it came free, with part of his ear, and he bit at it savagely for giving him so much pain, leaving tooth marks on its surface. His buttocks still hurt but the pain was dull and the blood had already stopped flowing.

On starting back towards the mountains he found the human trail was heading in the same direction and he felt the stirrings of fear within him for his mate. Humans hunting a tiger tend to be trigger-happy and do not stop to consider species or markings.

They sight a tiger, possibly just the flash of a striped coat moving from rock to rock, and they make assumptions. They do not stop to make deductions when a maneater is at large. They see, they kill. Simply that. Some of them probably did not even know there was more than one type of tiger.

He thought about his unborn cubs and panic tightened his mind. There was enough of the old thinking left to know that he had to reach her before they did.

He travelled fast, not pausing for rest or food and overtook them in a wide arc. They attacked in a noisy crowd as he was crossing the plain in front of them and came near to killing him this time. Only the high grasses saved him.

When they arrived at the foot of the mountains he let them know of his presence by walking through their camp at night, leaving his prints close to their beds. They had people watching all night, but no one saw him enter or leave. He recrossed the plains in the dawn, treading along a soft stream bank to give them an easy path to follow. Then he waited, on the jungle's edge, to let them have a sighting.

Unknown to him the foremost member of the group of hunters was approaching from another angle, and while he was standing offering a slim target to the main group, his profile was presented to this man, whose weapon sang just as the tiger caught his scent. A hole was burned through the fleshy part of his throat and he spun quickly for the trees.

When darkness came he limped his way towards the place of the tumbled-down stones, the temple that had frightened him when he first became a tiger with its smell of old deaths. It would be cool and dark inside.

The men came to the edge of the clearing just as he was climbing up the small, even steps. Inside were two large blocks, one bearing the shape of a man in stone. He settled beside this one, facing the door. Soon the sounds and scents of men were all around and he growled softly in his own throat, feeling the now familiar tenseness building up within his strong body. Then there was a man, just a small distance away, standing at the entrance, peering in at him. He kept very still, alert and ready to spring, his eyes on the man's eyes, waiting.

The man stared into the blackness of the room, his arm tipped with silver. The tiger could see the fear on the man's face, could smell it as it wafted into the enclosed space. There was no way of knowing if he was frightened of finding the tiger in the dark or whether it was the place itself that was the source of his dread.

The buzzing began again in Marillac's head. This time there was no stud to blame — no irritant to scratch with his claw.

The sound was accompanied by a deep throbbing. Warped images slid into the room, from dark corners and recesses.

At the tiger's shoulder the criss-cross scratches of *Harris* began to dance: in the doorway was a new Harris, who would kiss the marble of God's cold lips. And God would suck the life from his body: God, the tiger and spirit of Marillac. Drugged with the old ways, what was once a weak man was now strong. Marillac — heady with the scent of Steen's blood.

He turned his huge head to look up at God. The stone chest was pulsing slowly, the old stone heart moving in time to the tiger's own organ.

His eyes went back to the figure in the doorway. Gradually the man entered, letting his arm fall down by his side. He trod softly over the slime-thick floors until he stood before God, mesmerized as Marillac had been. The man was a thin, sickly creature. Did they honestly think Marillac could go back to a body like that? Steen had known, but Steen was wise in the ways of men.

Above, the stone eyes glinted triumphantly and the cold lips were wet with pleasure.

No, not yet, master, replied Marillac. *Let the others come to find him. Then, soon, there will be more and more. Now that we have one, there will always be others. Men cannot leave a mystery unsolved.*

A heavy atmosphere descended, thick with the heat and the cloying scent of God's breath.

You know we will serve you well. You gave her to me. They are your spawn.

Then came the sound of running feet on the steps outside.

"Peterson? Are you up there?"

The eyes of the man in the room remained on God's face.

"In here," he called.

As the room filled with the stink of evil, Marillac's claws eased out of their sheaths. God smiled and began uncurling his long, thin fingers. . . .

OUBLIETTE

"... the blue-black barrel of night
Beginning its slow, sure spiral, ascending
Through coils of years, wound dark on dark ..."
                                    C. B. Carey

question

am i a rat or a man?

this is the question that plagues my befuddled brain incessantly. if only the noise of the engines would cease perhaps i could learn to think with clarity but they thunder on, never pausing, and the wall which is also the floor vibrates, shaking my bones loose and rattling the teeth in my mouth. sometimes the question changes shape, but it is always there, in the dark, beside me.

i know there are physical differences between rats and men but i cannot remember perfectly what they are, any more than i can recall how i came to be in this place of darkness and sound. where did i come from? where am i now? what is this thing of flesh, bones and blood that houses a buzzing brain? darkness, noise and a curving prison of wet metal, these are the things i am sure of.

sometimes i believe that if i can manage to concentrate i will remember what i am, and i lie on the metal, my cheek next to its damp humming surface, but soon the strong vibrations make me stand again. i cannot keep my attention channelled in one direction long enough. it wanders, then i think, how am i standing, on four limbs or two? but the problem is not so easily solved — sometimes i find i am standing one way, sometimes the other. often i try to take all four limbs from the surface of the metal to escape the shaking that grinds my bones together beneath their thin covering of skin. to retain my sanity, i walk. i walk and run. forward movement is my one joy. i refuse to allow death to overtake me. i can outpace death by keeping ahead of it. it follows me, always, but death is a slow mover.

if i am a man, then i have lost my memory.
if i am rat then i have gained the power to reason.

accident

it was probably an accident. i blame everything on accidents. i have many accidents, in the dark, in the wet. i often slip and hurt myself, then i curse the water. but i know enough to realize that without the wetness i would thirst, and starve, because i eat the slime that the water grows. i lick it from the metal. it furs my tongue. occasionally i find a patch of slime that is wonderfully thick and i can eat away my stomach pains. sometimes i make a feast and gorge myself until the blood bangs hard in my head. i fall on the surface of the floor-wall and let the engines hammer at my skull until i can feel the stickiness of the blood running from my ears and nose, and the juddering shakes my teeth loose. then i get up and run and run, and scramble, until i can feel my heart pounding joyfulness into my veins and into my lean muscles.

theory

one time i thought i knew what it was, for i have hair on my body. i thought, *rats live in dark, cold places*. they need hair to protect them from the damp and cold. i wanted to be a rat. i still do. if i am a rat then one day i may get out of this place. one day the engines will stop and men will come to inspect, or clean, or service this part of their great machine and i will be set free. panels will open, there will be voices. and light. blessed light will enter in. sometime, sometime, there will be light.

if i am a man then i may never escape because i may be the one who fashioned this terrible machine. perhaps i have trapped myself inside my own invention? if this is so, there is no one to set me free. that first time i decided i was a rat i felt both relieved and happy. it seemed to make sense because my activities were all directed towards a decision to call myself a rat. i lived in a dark environment. i ran on four limbs. i licked sludge that grew on the surface of metal. these seemed to be the kind of things a rat would do. coupled with the fact that my body was covered in hair the answer seemed quite obvious. joyfully i threw myself into a fast-paced run, slipping and slithering on the algae and making rat noises with my mouth.

later, however, i realised that the hair could have grown *because* of the cold, since i had arrived in this place, to protect me from it. perhaps my body had changed to suit the conditions? it was possible i was blind and not in a place of absolute darkness. other possibilities crept in. i run on four limbs because it is easier on an uphill slope, and there is more grip on the slippery surface. i eat the algae because there is nothing else to eat. the answer was no answer. it fell away from me, as all the answers do.

but, discovering that my deductions are invalid does not make me a man. i am still something unknown, between two beasts — between two worlds.

sleep

the wall-floor is curved — concave — and behind beat the motors that allow me no sleep, no peace. i can only snatch dreams as i stand, for seconds at a time. my mind is a constant blur of thoughts, muzzy and singing with tautness. sometimes i fall down asleep and wake a short time later, shivering, cold and still deathly tired and being shuttled along the shallow stream by the vibration.

if i could stop the engines — if they would stop themselves — i would have a respite, a space, a period in which i could clear my mind of the noise. then i would have time to consider my position.

it's not only the lack of rest; there is also the aching of my body. the stiff joints. they all worry me constantly and vie independently for my attention. concentration is only possible when it is expended upon my pain, not my predicament. my pain is immediate. my situation requires afterthoughts. i have no energy for such luxuries.

dreams and monsters

i have had dreams that interfere with reality. i see things in the black around me. shapes. ugly forms. during those times i think i am a man, i hear rats scrambling eagerly away from my footsteps and i shudder because rats are repulsive creatures. when i am a rat i see the eyes of some hideous creature flash in dark — quickly. what? where? my heart races hard and terror blinds everything, even the pain. sometimes i try to make myself afraid, for when the fear is really on me i try to scratch my way through the walls and one day i might make it, before my finger-claws lose their hard tips, as they do, and the blood runs between them, sticky and warm.

there are some terrible things in dark places — beasts that cannot be imagined unless they are experienced. i have felt the fear clogging my throat, like a tumour, grown swiftly, so that i could not breathe — *dare not* breathe in case the monsters heard me and made me their companion for life. i do not fear death from them — i fear their embrace, their smiles at finding something in their lair to feed upon slowly with sickening *love*.

the worst times are when i smell stinking breath, coming from behind me, and i know the monsters are close. i dare not turn and see their forms, for i imagine ugly holes and oleaginous lumps, and the dripping of viscous fluids.

if i am a rat then i curse the substance, the phenomena that made me a quasi-intelligent creature. it may have been the engines. perhaps they radiate waves or produce some form of gas? perhaps the constant oscillations of the metal have shaken loose an hereditory clot in my brain making me a new kind of creature? maybe it is a side effect of my birth, being so near the engines? i list the questions but have no answers.

alternative theory

what if i am a man, trapped by my own or someone else's stupidity? what, say, if i was a man who had once been asked to crawl into the cavity walls of a spaceship, without my clothes to give me more freedom of movement in confined spaces: to prevent the kind of accidents that snagging clothes can cause? a maintenance man, sent in to repair a fault while the vehicle was in motion — the only survivor of a subsequent crash? this is my refragable nightmare. the vehicle now lies half-sunk in the swamps of an unexplored region — perhaps another world — and suture-thin cracks in the hull let in the air and dampness, allowing the slime to grow thick. the engines — ah, the engines! they keep hammering away, at idling speed, gathering their power from the sun's rays, awaiting a hand to switch them off. motors that roar and rattle in loosened mountings. motors that will continue to function while the sun still burns and their parts remain unworn, just turning over, at idling speed. and the exit doors are jammed, warped by the crash, hidden in the blackness.

this is a nightmare, elaborate yes, but constantly recurring. i could choose it as a basis for truth, except that there are other dreams, just as fanciful, just as logical. dreams of sea ships, of being sealed inside after the last welder has joined the final plates with mucoid silver. dreams of being a rat inside a metal coffin, with no way out. a moebius strip — a single side and no entrance or exit, neither a beginning nor an end. just a wall turning into a wall. this is another nightmare.

further theories

the worst nightmare of all is the experiment dream. (notice the thread running through all these dreams? the ships? the movement through space or liquid? somewhere there is a clue which i cannot grasp tightly enough in order to inspect it. there are many things i am aware of which i should have forgotten with the rest — why do i know metal? or the name for the slime, algae? — not only do i know the name, i know the colour, which is green! pieces of knowledge, small pieces with jagged, irregular edges that do not fit together, that are not uniform, are scattered like shards in my buried brain.)

but the experiment dream: that hardly bears telling. consider this: i was a rat in a sewer and was trapped by man. man wished to go out into space, but he did not dare because he feared that his mind might not stand up to the psychological stresses. so he operated on a rat, with instruments and drugs, until that rat was intelligent and not only did it think *like* a man — it believed it was a man. it had to, for the experiment to be a success.

they sent the rat out in one of their spaceships, and when the drugs wore off, it was there, alone, in a craft that hurtled through suns and suns. it was a man, yet physically a rat. but it did not remember being a rat, for it was not intelligent then. it believed only that it was a man and it had no reason to doubt that, no reason to question it. then, on the return journey, they tell it — they tell *me* — i am a rat which, as i think like a man, i know is a loathesome creature that haunts the filth of human waste, and walks with disease for a companion. the shock is unbearable.

listen to your voice, they say. is that a human sound? and i want to see them, see their shape, and i punch out the request on the communicator, but they refuse. i read the words *request denied* and i wonder if they are lying to me — i wonder if those that sent me are no longer in control and those that have taken over wish the experiment to fail and want to drive me insane. how can i be a rat when i am a man? i try to destroy myself and the ship, the hate bubbling from my mouth at the terrible trick they have played on me. the subsequent crash is not successful. i am trapped inside my vehicle.

i wake in the dark, trembling with fright and still unsure of whether i am indeed a man — or whether the dream is true and those words upon the screen were the truth. if only i could remember what a man looked like — or what form a rat took — then i would be free, even in here.

i increase my pace, for even as i was dreaming, i was moving, stumbling forward. i break into a semi-joyous run. it is the only way to dispel the depression, the hopelessness. recently, however, my movements have become more lethargic. the pain in my body has given way to a strange kind of numbness, it is almost as if i am changing state, solid to liquid, liquid to gas . . .

sickness

i am sick. i think i am dying. death is at last gnawing at the heels it has pursued for so long. now i cannot move, my limbs are too weak to raise my body. i lie for what seems an eternity, my limp form shrugged along the uncaring, wet, metal womb. now i know i shall never escape, never be free again — *again?* was i ever free? did i ever taste sunlight and sweet air, or are those fanciful inventions of a mind trapped in a dark enclosure? i lie here and time passes, the buzzing of my brain increasing in volume, the pain in my head intense. time. time.

listen!

listen .

i can hear. i can hear noises which do not come from the engines.

the engines have stopped!

there is something outside the wall. a banging — a scraping and shuffling. i can hear it! who are they?

will they be rats, or men? they must be men, for rats cannot use tools. perhaps they are men who look like rats, or rats in the disguise of men? my brain spins, clicking through all the combinations, finding no set of letters which reveal the secret to my existence.

unless! — unless i am on another place, another world where things are not the same. where the intelligent life does not know, does not care, what the shell is like that carries the brain. perhaps it cares only that i too am a sentient being? on a place like that my form would make no difference.

listen! is the noise one of rescue? they are trying to enter, yet they do not speak to one another. i can only hear the sound of metal against metal.

release

i lean against the cool metal, still now, and quiet. it is a soothing coolness and i stay there a long time, until i see a glow, a dim haze of light, and someone or something, is lowered into the chamber and lies beside me, fast asleep. what is this new creature? a companion for me? yet i am dying. they must know i am dying. this is not a companion but a replacement. i feel their eyes upon me. *damn you, i am not yet dead. leave me to go in peace.*

the glow disappears. there is blackness again. i drift into death with flimsy thoughts like ghosts evaporating into the darkness around me. i will never know. i do not wish to know. i hear a breathing somewhere near me, shallow breathing, the sound of drugged sleep. as the last vestiges of mortality leave my body i hear the breath quicken. then a cry, and movement. feet begin to pad against the metal surface. there is the sound of running, scrambling, running. suddenly, the engines rumble to life again ... in here there is darkness, but someone, somewhere, has light.

THE SONGBIRDS OF PAIN

Tomorrow they would break her legs.

At first, every morning, there were songbirds in the fire trees outside her hospital window and every evening the frogs sang in the storm drains with choirs of bass voices. (Not when she woke or went to sleep: in her twilight world of pain there was no real sleep, just a clinging to the edge of a dream, an intermittent misting of the brain.) Then there came a time when the birds and frogs seemed to be singing from within her, deep within her flesh, her bones. The pitch of their notes was, on occasion, as sharp as thorns; and at other times as dull as small hammer blows on a hollow skull. Her world was full of the agony of their music: the songbirds of Brazil entered her blood and swam with slow wings the channels of her body. The tree-frogs, the ground-frogs, they also filled the long, narrow passages of her limbs, her breasts and her mind with their melodies. If snakes could sing they would have been there too, accompanying the cicadas and grasshoppers; the rhythmic, ticking beetles; even high-singing bats and clicking lizards.

She tried to remember the time when all these songsters, these choral wonders of an exotic land, were not part of her, were separate from her. There was a man, somewhere, who led her to this state. If she could remember . . .

Philip would indulge her, she knew, to the extent of his fortune. Anita's approach, however, was cautious, because of the nature of her request. Even so, the amount of money involved was considerable and, as was his habit, he reached for the whisky when he was thrown off-balance. She had come to realize that it was not the alcohol that was the crutch but the need to hold something in his hand, upon which he could concentrate while he recovered his composure. The worst was yet to come. She waited until he had poured his drink and was gripping the glass.

"Yes —," she mentioned the sum — "it's a lot of money, I know, but I'll give up a few things ... my fur coat, this flat. ..."

He looked up sharply. "The flat? Where will you live? You're not moving out of London? What do you want this money *for*?"

She hesitated before replying. It was difficult to tell someone you needed a great deal of money in order to have all your bones broken. It would sound ridiculous. Perhaps it *was* ridiculous.

"I'll have to go away ... it's an operation. Don't look so alarmed, I'm not ill or anything."

He frowned, rolling the crystal tumbler slowly between his palms. Anita wondered whether Philip's wife was aware of this trait: she liked to think she could read this man better than Marjorie but perhaps that was arrogance, conceit? Perhaps Marjorie was aware of more important supports than whisky glasses. Like mistresses.

"Cosmetic surgery? But you're already beautiful. I like you the way you are. Why should you want to change?"

"It's more than that, Philip. Something I can't really explain ... I'm twenty-six. In a few more years my present ... looks will begin to fade. I need a beauty that will remain outstanding. It's all I have. I'm not clever, like you. Nor do I have the kind of personality that Marjorie possesses. You both have a charisma that goes deeper than looks. It may be something superficial that I'm searching for but I do need it ... I want to make the *best* of myself. If I'm beautiful to begin with, then that just means that I need less improvement — but there is a great deal of me I want improved."

"Where will you go? Where is this place, the USA?"

She shook her head. Perhaps this was one time he would refuse her adamantly. In which case she would have to bide her time, wait for another lover, just as wealthy, but more willing to indulge her.

Yet she knew she could not leave this man. She loved him much too deeply.

"Brazil. A town on the edge of the jungle called Algarez. There's a surgeon there ... I would trust him. It's a difficult operation but I know he's carried it out on two other women. It was very successful."

"Brazil?" Again, the rolling of the glass, the slight frown of disapproval. She knew that his business interests would not allow him the time to travel at this point in the calendar. She would have to go alone. "Do I know either of these women?"

"One of them. Sarah Shields."

"The actress. But my God, she was unrecognizable when she returned to society. I mean, she looked nothing like her former self — extremely beautiful, yes, but...."

Anita suddenly wanted to knock the glass out of his hand. Sometimes he lacked the understanding of which she knew he was capable.

"... beautiful, yes, *but*...." There were no *buts* to Anita. Everything was contained in one word. Beauty. She wanted it badly. *Real* beauty, not just a passable beauty. To be the most...

"Will you help me?" she asked simply.

He looked into her eyes and suddenly he smiled. A wonderful, understanding smile and she knew it would be all right. Philip was usually the most generous of men, but there was that protective shield around his heart, wine-glass thin but resistant nonetheless, which she had to shatter gently at times. It was not just the large issues, like this, which revealed the fragile shell that encapsulated his *givingness*, but small things too — like a trip to the art gallery or the reading of a poem to her while they lay in bed after making love. It was something to do with his fear of being manipulated, something concerned with defending that part of his ego which abhorred control. She knew he needed her, but not as much as she needed him — in fact her own need reached desperation point at times and she resented the fact that his, though apparent, was not as consuming as her own. Anita thought, suddenly, of his wife. She had never been jealous of Marjorie. Anyone else, yes, but Marjorie was his wife and, more important, she came *before* Anita.

"When will you leave?" he asked.

"Next month," she replied.

Anita went into the kitchen to make some coffee while Philip finished his whisky. As she made the coffee she considered the forthcoming trip. Travel was now one of her greatest enjoyments, although this had not always been the case. Brazil. She wondered whether she would like it there. She remembered her first visit abroad, how awful it had been. Normandy, as a young girl on a school exchange. It had been a depressing visit. The family she stayed with insisted on impressing her with trips to the war graves — rows and rows of white crosses. Strange, she thought, that men who had died in such chaos should be buried in neat, symmetrical lines, while conversely, men who had lived quiet, orderly lives — bankers, stockbrokers, insurance people — usually ended up in untidy graveyards, their headstones looking as if they had been planted by some blind maladroit giant.

She shook off the thoughts of death. After all, it was not death that awaited her in Brazil, but fulfilment, albeit that the road to that end was paved with pain. She knew it was going to be hard but it was a rebirth that was worth the agony she would have to endure. She hoped her mind was strong enough. Until Philip met her she had been a shop assistant. At twenty he had persuaded her to take up a career in modelling so that she could travel with the small fashion house he financed, and they could be together more often. She was now twenty-six and wiser only in a world as seen through Philip's eyes. He had kept her closeted, comfortable and happy for four years. Her opinions were second-hand and originally his. She realized this had created an insipid personality but for the present she was satisfied with the status quo. Later, when she had lost him (as she was bound to do one day), perhaps she could develop her own identity.

Of Philip's former life, she knew only the surface details. He had married at twenty-five while in the process of clawing his way to the first ledge on the cliff of success. Success, in Philip's terms, was money and certain pleasures that went with it. He was a considerate lover and good to his wife in all things but absolute fidelity. He was not a philanderer. Also he did not squander money on luxuries he did not really require, like yachts, cars and swimming pools. He had one of everything he needed except . . . except women. The thought jarred when she reduced it to those terms. There was a certain greed associated with his wants which she generously connected with insecurity. The truth probably lay somewhere in between those two character defects. His had not been an easy climb either. He had come from a poor background. Philip had since acquired considerable polish and was thought of by his contemporaries as an aristocratic businessman rather than working class, *nouveau riche*.

At the time Anita had met him, he had been thirty-two. He had given her a lift home after work at a store for which he supplied new fashions. Now she was making coffee for him following an evening at the theatre and before he went home to his wife.

She took in the coffee and they drank it in silence. They would not make love tonight. Sex was not the most important part of their relationship, in any case. Philip needed her more for the affection she gave him. Not that Marjorie was unaffectionate, but Anita had come to know that, while Philip was a tough businessman, he was privately very sentimental and needed a great deal of emotional support. It provided the background softness to a life full of hard-bitten decisions. Neither woman was volatile or demonstrative. They were both warm and loyal, with loving dispositions. It was not contrasts Philip required but additions. In turn, he gave much — almost as much as either woman asked for — in both practical and emotional terms.

"I'll have to be getting home now," he said, after the coffee. She nodded. "I know."

"I'm sorry. I'd like to stay tonight but Marjorie's expecting me."

"It's all right, Philip, really it is. I'm fine. I've got a good book and the television if I need it. Please don't worry."

He kissed her gently on the brow and she stood up and fetched his coat.

"I'll call you," he said, standing at the door.

"I'll be here." He never could say goodbye, always using feeble excuses, like a just-remembered something or other, to prolong the final parting for the night. Even a half-closed door was not a sure indication that he was on his way. He might turn at the last minute, whip off his coat and say, "Dammit, another hour won't hurt. I'll say the car had a flat or something."

"Go, Philip," she said. "Just *go*."

He shrugged huffily inside his overcoat and stepped on to the landing. She closed the door and then went into the living-room to clear away the coffee things. She carried them into the kitchen but as she placed the tray on the working surface, her arm knocked over the percolator, which was still on. Hot coffee splashed on to her leg and the pain sent her reeling backwards.

"Philip!" she cried.

She inspected herself. There was a red weal the size of a handprint on her thigh, as if she had been slapped hard.

Philip. Damn him. He was never there when he was needed most. That was one of the disadvantages of being a kept woman. The partner was not on call. *Christ, that hurts,* she thought. She put her leg under the cold tap and turned it on. The water would bring down her skin temperature. Afterwards, she felt a little better, and took several aspirins before crawling into bed. Funny, she thought, lying in bed, when she was a child they said the worst thing one could do with a burn was put cold water on it. A dry bandage was the recommended treatment. Now, *they,* whoever *they* were, had decided to reverse the treatment completely. The world was controlled by whims. The last thing she remembered before she fell asleep was that her leg still hurt her.

The flight to Brasilia was long and uncomfortable but Anita was excited, not only by the thought of the impending operation, but by the idea of being in South America.

She made her visits during the next day and took in the night life of the city in the evening. There was no real enjoyment in it for her though, because she wanted to share it all with Philip, and he was several thousand miles away. She telephoned him but the instrument had always been impersonal to her. She could not feel close to him, even while she was listening to his vaguely distorted voice.

"Philip ... it's Anita."

An echo of her voice followed each word and then a long, deep silence in which it seemed to her that the ears of all the world were tuned in to their private conversation.

"... lo, darling, ... are you?" Parts of his speech were lost to her. It was a distressing business. She wanted to reach out and touch him, not exchange banalities over thousands of miles. Damn, what was that clicking? She could not hear him properly.

"Fine, everything's fine," she said. It sounded hollow, flat. There was more of the same.

"Look after yourself," he finished, after a very unsatisfactory five minutes. When she replaced the receiver she felt further away from him than before the call had begun. Hell, it was supposed to bring them closer, not emphasize the vast distance that separated them. She needed him desperately. If she had asked him, he would have come running, but there was no real excuse — not one of which he would approve. Just a longing for his company which was almost a physical hurt inside her.

The flight to the hospital, over the dark green back of prehistoric jungles, was short but not uneventful. They flew low enough in the small aircraft for her to study the moody rivers, the sudden clearings studded with huts, the forests pressing down a personal night beneath their impenetrable layers of foliage. Down there were big cats, deadly snakes and spiders the size of soup plates, and alligators with skins like tank tracks.

On landing, she went straight to the hospital. It was a small white building on the outskirts of the town, surrounded by gardens with trees of brilliant hues. The colour of the blossoms was so light and buoyant it seemed that only the buried roots held the splendid trees to the earth: should the roots be severed, they would rise slowly like balloons, to take her up into the atmosphere.

Anita's fanciful thoughts, she knew, stemmed from her desire to steer herself away from considering the forthcoming operation. When she was confronted by the surgeon, however, she knew she would have to face up to the ordeal. His office was on the second floor. He had switched off his air conditioner and flung windows and balcony doors open wide, letting in the smell of vegetation. She could see out, over the balcony and beyond the hospital gardens. The light seemed to gather near the edge of the dark jungle, as if the forest perimeter was a dam to hold back the day, to stop its bright wave rolling in to defile the old trees and ancient, overgrown temples.

The surgeon spoke; his words, perhaps subconsciously, were timed exactly to coincide with the metronome clicking of the auxiliary overhead fan.

"You realize," he said, "there will be a great deal of pain." He was an elderly American with a soft accent and gentle eyes but she had difficulty in not looking down at his hands. Those narrow fingers, as white as driftwood with continual scrubbing, would soon be cracking her bones. They were strong-looking hands, and the arms to which they were joined, powerful. Many limbs had been purposefully broken with cold, calculated accuracy, by those hands.

"We can only give you drugs up to a certain point. The whole operation is a long business — a series of operations in fact — and we don't want to send you out a morphine addict."

She nodded. "I understand."

What sort of instruments are used? she wanted to ask, but was too afraid of the answer actually to do so. She imagined ugly steel clamps, vices and mechanical hammers that were fitted with a precision more suited to a factory jig than a medical instrument. This is the way we break your bones. *We screw this here, that there — can you feel the cold metal against your skin? The plates gripping the bone? — then, once we have lined it up and in position — whap! — down comes the weight between the guide blocks and* crack! *goes the bone. Easy, isn't it?*

"Of course, once we're finished with you, you will be ... ah, even more beautiful than you can imagine."

"That's what I want. I don't care about the pain so long as the result is good."

"Not *good*, but *breathtaking*. We'll straighten out any defects in the limbs, give you a jaw-line that Cleopatra would envy, small feet, slender hands. We'll also graft a little flesh here and there. Take away any excess. The eyes, we can do much with the eyes. And we'll have to break those fingers, one or two of them ... am I being too blunt?"

"No, no." She had paled, she knew, at the word *break*. The other words were fine. She could take terms like "*straighten the limbs*" — but *break* had a force behind it which shook her confidence.

"I'll be all right," she said. "It must be the journey, the heat or something. Please don't worry. Please go on."

Her body was alive with feeling, as if electricity were coursing through her veins instead of blood. She concentrated on his words as he began to describe what her experiences would be, to ensure, he said, that she knew *exactly* what to expect. If she wished, she could leave now and there would be no charge.

Outside the window, the birds were singing and she concentrated not on his descriptions of the forthcoming mutilations of her body, but on their songs.

* * *

At first the pain was a patchy, dull feeling, its location in her body specific to certain areas, like her forearms, which were the first to be broken. An aching that was difficult but not impossible to bear. At night, when she was left alone, she could feel the pain throbbing and pulsing in the various parts of her limbs. Later, it developed a sharpness, and spread like a field-fire through her whole anatomy, until there was no pinpointing its source. The pain was her, she was the pain. It reached a pitch and intensity that filled her with a terror she had never before thought possible. Could not have imagined in her worst nightmares. It had shape, and form, and had become a tangible thing that had banished her psyche, had taken over completely her whole being. There was nothing inside her skin but the beast pain: no heart, no brain, no flesh, no bones, no soul. Just the beast. It was *unbearable* and she refused to bear it. She tried, with all her willpower, to remove it from her body. It was then that the pain began to sing to her. It called in the birds from beneath their waxen leaves, the fabric blossoms: it summoned the night singers, the small green tree-frogs and the booming bulls from their mudbank trumpets; it persuaded the chit-chat lizards to enter in, and the insects to abandon the bladed grasses for its sake. When it had gathered together its choirs, the beast pain sang to her. It sang unholy hymns with mouths of needle teeth, and the birds, frogs and insects sang its song. Gradually, over the many days, she felt the sharp sweetness of their music giving her a new awareness, lifting her to a new, higher plane of experience, until there came a time when she was dependent upon their presence.

Tomorrow they would break her legs. She lay back in her bed, unable to move her head because of the clamps on her jaw. Her arms were completely healed. The plaster had left them pale and thin, with her skin flaking off, but the doctor assured her they would soon look normal. Better than normal, of course. Then her jaw had been reshaped. That was *almost* healed. The surgeon was insistent she wait for her legs to be remodelled, even though she told him she wanted the process hurried so that she could get back to Philip. *Her legs.* She knew the worst pain was yet to come. Then, of course, there were the minor operations; her nose, fingers, toes and ears. (Afterwards she could wear her hair shorter. Would not need to cover those ugly ears, which would then be beautiful.) The surgeon had also mentioned scraping away some of the bone above her eyes, where there were slight bulges. (She had never noticed them, but he had obviously done so.) Also there were her shoulder blades to adjust — the scapulae — she was even beginning to learn the Latin names. . . .

Sweet pain! What delicious strains came from its small mouths. Sing to me, she whispered, *sing! She needed more, and more.*

"The hands haven't gone too well, we're going to have to re-work them," he said.

She smiled, as much as the wire brace would allow.

"If you have to."

"You're a brave woman."

"I try to be," she replied, drifting off into her other world, the *real* world, where she became herself. Her actual *self*.

In there, deep inside, lay the quintessential spark of being, where she was pure *Anita*. To reach that spark, it was necessary to use an agent — drugs, medication, will, faith, religion, or perhaps *pain*. Pain was her vehicle to that interior world, that inscape which made the rest of life seem a wasteland of experience. There was the power, the energy of birth. The cold release of death. Heady. Unequivocally the centre of the universe. So strange to find that all else revolved around her. That nothing existed that was not derived from her. Even Philip. She *was* the sun, the moon, the stars, the Earth. She was void, she was matter, she was light.

Anita and her pain.

"How do you feel?" asked the surgeon.

She smiled. "Like a new woman. How do I look?"

"See for yourself. . . ." He indicated the mirror on the wall but she had already studied herself for hours before the mirror in her room. The scars were now invisible, the blemishes and bruises gone. Blue-black skin had been replaced by her normal cream complexion. And now? Now her features were . . . breathtaking, yes. Her whole body was perfect in its proportions. This was what she had desired for many years. Beauty, absolute.

"I'm very pleased," she said. "I really haven't the words to express my thanks."

He held up a hand. "I've been adequately rewarded," he said.

"We don't do it for love of beauty — although I admit to being proud of my art. And I must congratulate you on your courage. You withstood the pain with as much bravery as I've ever seen."

She shrugged. "It isn't something I'd like to go through again," she lied, "but I think it's been worth it. It *has* been worth it," she hastily amended.

They shook hands.

"You're a very beautiful woman," he said, in a voice that suggested he had forgotten he had created her.

On the drive away, she barely looked at the trees, still dripping with colours. Their blooms no longer interested her. Nor the birds upon their branches. She had her own colours, her own songbirds.

Philip was waiting by the exit of the airport arrival lounge. She saw him from the far side of the room. He was looking directly at her and she realized that he did not recognize her. He looked away and began searching the faces of the other passengers.

She began walking towards him. Twice more he looked at her, as if expecting a sign from her to tell him she was Anita, then back to the other passengers. She noticed his expression was expectant but calm. He thought he had no need to be anxious. Anita was supposed to declare herself. As she drew closer she *almost* wavered in her purpose.

Her heart flooded with emotion. God, he was her *life*. Never would she have the same feelings for any other man. He was everything to her. Philip. Even the name was enough to fill her heart with the desire, the passion, the tender feelings of love. She needed him, wanted him above all else except. . . .

She studied his eyes, his face, his quizzical expression as she passed him and then went through the exit, her feelings choking her. She was leaving him. She wanted him desperately, but she was leaving him — and the delicious pain, the emotional agony was exquisite. She nurtured the hurt inside her, listening to the music that ran through her veins. This was beauty: the delight, the ecstasy of spiritual pain, even sweeter than a physical hurt. Her songbirds would be with her till death, and her indulgence in the music they created washed through her whole being, and made her complete, made the whole of existence complete, for everyone — even Philip.

Also available from Unwin Paperbacks

THEATRE OF TIMESMITHS
Garry Kilworth

Trapped behind walls of towering ice, First City was a prison from which no one ever escaped. The trysts ruled with an iron fist: violent death was a common sight on the streets.

Morag MacKenzie was a mind-prostitute who gave erotic thought-stimulation, without giving her body. Those who yearned for other escapes visited the Timesmiths, within whose hands time could be moulded like clay as they spun dream-visions. But Morag has her own dreams, of a world outside the ice walls, a world of space and freedom, and she is determined to find it.

'Great SF . . . a wonderfully inventive story.'
World of Books Magazine

'A fine novel.'
Punch

'A convincing display of talent.'
The Times

'Garry Kilworth . . . is in the first rank of British SF writers, with Aldiss and Roberts and Ballard.'
Newsagent And Bookshop

CLOUDROCK
Garry Kilworth

On Cloudrock the penalty for imperfection is death: death by the long fall into the void, through the poisonous mists and gases that rise from the deadlands far, far below. The two tribes who survive on the Rock, the tribes of Day and Night, keep their families tight, their bloodlines pure and true, by incest, by cannibalism and by murder. Parcelling out their tiny world in measures of light and time, they wrap themselves in ritual and taboo, each family denying the presence of the other.

Then came the Shadow.

Born to the matriarch Catrunner, the Shadow is deformed – a neuter dwarf – a natural candidate for instant death. But for this mutant, fate intervenes. The Shadow may live – on the condition that none acknowledge its presence: one word, one glance, and the Shadow will join its luckless kin in the long death-flight.

Surviving on the outskirts of the family, the Shadow's very existence creates an unspoken question that challenges the ties that bind.

This is the Shadow's tale.

THE ICE MONKEY
M. John Harrison

The world of *The Ice Monkey* is a dangerous place, which steals over you like a dream. It is a twilight world of stark cities, doomed humanity, bizarre rites and psychic horrors. Powerful and unsettling, this collection established M. John Harrison as a distinctive and significant voice in contemporary fiction.

'Harrison's imagination is merciless. His fiction is a scalpel slicing through the skin of the world to make dissections both strange and disturbingly familiar. This collection puts him in the company of Ian McEwan and Peter Carey, but he is grittier than Carey and wittier than McEwan.'   *Times Literary Supplement*

'. . . a sharpness of detail and sureness of overall control that is wholly admirable . . . writing of remarkable resonance and power.'   *London Review of Books*

'M. John Harrison is the finest British writer now writing horror fiction and by far the most original.'
Ramsey Campbell

'Stylish, accomplished, evocative short stories, exemplary fictions of unease shot through with poetic insights and most beautifully written.'   *Angela Carter*

'Overpowering'   *Punch*

'. . . material handled with a grace that approaches the mandarin . . . A brief review can only serve to indicate the richness of this book if taken as a whole . . . Mr Harrison's progress becomes fascinating.'
Robert Nye. *The Guardian*

OTHER EDENS
Edited by Christopher Evans and Robert Holdstock

Sixteen fantasy and science fiction tales from established British-based writers including Garry Kilworth, M. John Harrison, Tanith Lee, Brian Aldiss, Michael Moorcock, Keith Roberts, Lisa Tuttle and Ian Watson.

Take a flight of the imagination to distant planets, future worlds, other Edens; through mysteries ancient and modern, dark rituals, spine-chilling hauntings and creatures made from human flesh, and travel beyond the stars, to the enigmas of science and time, and man's eternal battle for survival and for power.

'The whole collection is excellent value.'
New Statesman

'Although the theme is science fiction and fantasy the contributors to this original anthology are all imaginative story-tellers in their own right and the tales can be enjoyed by the general reader, as well as the specialist.'
Echo

'Marvellous stories ... four of these are absolutely brilliant, the rest only very good ... highly recommended.' *Birmingham Science Fiction Group*

'... a collection of quality writing.'
Terry Greer

Also available from Unwin Paperbacks

The Armies of Daylight (The Darwath Trilogy: 3)	
Barbara Hambly	£2.95 ☐
The Darkest Road (The Fionavar Tapestry: 3) *Guy Kay*	£2.95 ☐
The Deep *John Crowley*	£2.95 ☐
Dragonsbane *Barbara Hambly*	£2.95 ☐
Freedom Beach *James Patrick Kelly & John Kessel*	£2.95 ☐
The Ice Monkey *M. John Harrison*	£2.95 ☐
The Initiate (The Time Master Trilogy: 1) *Louise Cooper*	£2.95 ☐
In Viriconium *M. John Harrison*	£2.95 ☐
The Ladies of Mandrigyn *Barbara Hambly*	£2.95 ☐
The Master (The Time Master Trilogy: 3) *Louise Cooper*	£2.95 ☐
Mirage *Louise Cooper*	£2.95 ☐
Other Edens *ed. Christopher Evans & Robert Holdstock*	£2.95 ☐
The Outcast (The Time Master Trilogy: 2) *Louise Cooper*	£2.95 ☐
The Pastel City *M. John Harrison*	£2.50 ☐
Prince of Stars *Ian Dennis*	£2.95 ☐
The Silent Tower *Barbara Hambly*	£2.95 ☐
The Silicon Mage *Barbara Hambly*	£2.95 ☐
A Storm of Wings *M. John Harrison*	£2.95 ☐
The Summer Tree (The Fionavar Tapestry: 1) *Guy Kay*	£2.95 ☐
Theatre of Timesmiths *Garry Kilworth*	£2.95 ☐
The Time of the Dark (The Darwath Trilogy: 1)	
Barbara Hambly	£2.95 ☐
Viriconium Nights *M. John Harrison*	£2.95 ☐
Walls of Air (The Darwath Trilogy: 2) *Barbara Hambly*	£2.95 ☐
The Wandering Fire (The Fionavar Tapestry: 2) *Guy Kay*	£2.95 ☐
The Witches of Wenshar *Barbara Hambly*	£2.95 ☐

All these books are available at your local bookshop or newsagent, or can be ordered direct by post. Just tick the titles you want and fill in the form below.

Name ....

Address ....

....

....

Write to Unwin Cash Sales, PO Box 11, Falmouth, Cornwall TR10 9EN.

Please enclose remittance to the value of the cover price plus:

UK: 60p for the first book plus 25p for the second book, thereafter, 15p for each additional book ordered to a maximum charge of £1.90.

BFPO and EIRE: 60p for the first book plus 25p for the second book and 15p for the next 7 books and thereafter 9p per book.

OVERSEAS INCLUDING EIRE: £1.25 for the first book plus 75p for the second book and 28p for each additional book.

Unwin Paperbacks reserve the right to show new retail prices on covers which may differ from those previously advertised in the text or elsewhere. Postage rates are also subject to revision.